Colin rolled
"So what *do* y~~ou want to do now?~~"

A dozen images jumped immediately to mind, and she gritted her teeth to keep from describing them in detail. "I guess we could go back to the Quarter? After all you've said about it I'm kinda curious to see the insanity for myself."

He looked doubtful. "Are you sure?"

No, but you're not giving me any better options. "Isn't it part of the full Mardi Gras experience?"

"Oh, honey, it's an experience all its own." He leaned all the way back, stacking his hands behind his head. Turning his head toward her, he arched an eyebrow. "You think you can handle it?"

"I don't think I'm that shockable."

That earned her a smile. "Then let's do it."

He rolled to his feet and brushed the grass off before extending a hand to help her up. The crowds weren't quite as thick here, so Colin didn't take her hand—sadly—but he did put his hand on the small of her back to guide her. She was so primed even that simple touch was downright torture.

Dear Reader

Just one more book set in New Orleans and then I'll stop. Or maybe I won't. It's a tough call, since I love New Orleans *and* it seems to be the perfect setting for a romance. New Orleans is exciting and vibrant and sexy, not afraid to break rules, push boundaries, or do its own thing its own way. It's hard to resist and too much is never enough.

Kinda like a Modern Tempted™, you know... *~grin~*

After years of insisting that he's *totally* the inspiration for the heroes in my books, this time my Darling Geek will actually be telling the truth. In many ways Colin is based on my Geek, and at least one of the conversations between Colin and Jamie happened in real life—all I had to do was transcribe it. I'm not a Girl Geek—I don't know a sonic screwdriver from a warp drive—but I *am* a geek girl. I go geeky for geeks. They rock my world.

And if indulging my love for New Orleans and geeks in this book wasn't enough to make me smile, I also got to work with the fabulous Aimee Carson again on this duet. Aimee's great; everyone should brainstorm with her. I loved having Aimee's heroine, Callie, guest star in this book, and I know you're going to love getting to know her better in her story.

There's so much *I* love about this book—I just hope *you'll* love Colin and Jamie's story as well.

As always, I hope you'll find me on Facebook, Twitter or my website (www.BooksByKimberly.com) and stay in touch! I'd love to hear from you.

Love

Kimberly

NO TIME LIKE
MARDI GRAS

BY
KIMBERLY LANG

MILLS
BOON®

Kimberly Lang hid romance novels behind her textbooks in junior high, and even a Master's programme in English couldn't break her obsession with dashing heroes and happily-ever-after. A ballet dancer turned English teacher, Kimberly married an electrical engineer and turned her life into an ongoing episode of *When Dilbert Met Frasier*. She and her Darling Geek live in beautiful North Alabama, with their one Amazing Child—who, unfortunately, shows an aptitude for sports.

Visit Kimberly at www.booksbykimberly.com for the latest news—and don't forget to say hi while you're there!

To Finlay, you gorgeous, clever boy. I know you're going to grow up to be even more awesome than you are now. (And remember your auntie knows a thing or two about awesome men, so you can trust me on that!)

PROLOGUE

From *The Ex Factor:*

Dear Exes,
My ex and I were together for three years and knew
each other socially before that. Unfortunately, while
our relationship is over, I still see him all the time.
We have the same friends, go to the same places…
it's really awkward. We don't hate each other, but
we don't want to be together anymore. How should
I handle this?

Callie:

It takes time and a bit of tact. You don't want to
alienate your friends or make them feel as though
they have to choose one of you and exclude the
other. Change what habits and haunts you can—
find a new coffee shop, a new bar to hang out in—
so that the old places don't remind you or others of
your former couple status. Your friends will take
their cues from you, so the more over him you are
and the more comfortable you are in his presence,
the easier it will become for everyone. You might
even want to do things in smaller groups—minus

your ex, of course—until the breakup isn't so fresh. Eventually those friend-only feelings will return.

Ex-Man:

Move. As far away as you possibly can. I cannot recommend this strongly enough. You can always make new friends.

CHAPTER ONE

SOMETIMES BEING A *nice guy sucked*.

But a friend didn't turn down a friend in need, even when that need was for a relief bartender on Fat Tuesday in the French Quarter.

Seemed he'd only *thought* his bartending days were over. And he'd forgotten how much he hated bartending.

Colin Raine made another cash drop just as Teddy came downstairs from his apartment above the Lucky Gator, looking somewhat better rested and fresh from the shower. Owning a bar in the French Quarter had been Teddy's dream, but the frenetic, nearly twenty-four-seven nature of the business during Mardi Gras would test even the most pleasant of dreams come true. The guy hadn't had more than a couple of hours' sleep in a row all weekend.

"All good?" Teddy asked.

"All good." Colin usually avoided the Quarter on Fat Tuesday—at least since bartending had quit being his main source of income—far preferring to watch the parades over near his own place off Lee Circle or hang with friends. At least it was still early, only just past noon, and while the revelers were thick in the streets, he had time to escape before the crowds really got crazy. "You owe me, though. Some drunk frat rat puked in the men's."

Teddy rolled his eyes. "Already?"

First-time visitors to the Quarter on Fat Tuesday always faced a bit of a shock at the all-out, truly bacchanalian atmosphere. Half the people on the streets were still drunk from the night before, and the rest were rushing to catch up. Depending on perspective, it was either the biggest and best street party in the world or an absolute nightmare.

The Lucky Gator occupied a great piece of real estate, just a block in from Canal on Chartres, and the place was hopping simply from the traffic of folks heading into or out of the Quarter itself or trickling in from the parade route on Canal. A local cover band played with enthusiasm—if not extreme skill—on the Gator's small stage, calling folks in off the streets to continue the party indoors. Every table was occupied and folks stood in the doorways. They weren't packed yet, but they would be— the crowds were already starting to pick up. Teddy was making a mint, which tended to dull the irritation of those who were letting the *bons temps rouler* a little *too* much.

He helped Teddy restock and bring out new kegs, dumped his share of the morning's tips into the beleaguered waitresses' tip jar, and took out the trash, where he was waylaid by the stupidity of two women who'd thought flashing for beads at street level was a good idea. It took him ten minutes to get them out of the groping maw of an overly appreciative crowd that looked as if it could easily turn aggressive and on their way with their friends.

With that, though, his good deeds for the day were officially done. He was getting the hell out of here. He had time for a shower and a nap before deciding if he'd head to a party or just stay home and work.

He went to tell Teddy that exact thing, only to find him staring oddly at something near the stage. Colin followed

Teddy's line of sight and nodded. "She's been there for a couple of hours now."

"She doesn't look happy about it."

The she in question was a pretty brunette, maybe in her mid-twenties, scrolling idly through her phone. While the other woman at the table, a blonde, was turned around, straddling her chair, practically dancing in her seat and catcalling the band, the brunette looked, for lack of a better word, bored. She had a couple of strands of beads around her neck and a beer he'd pulled over an hour ago sitting untouched on the table in front of her. It was a stark contrast to the scene surrounding her. She put her phone back in her pocket and seemed to sigh as she turned to watch the street.

Teddy shook his head. "A reluctant groupie."

Colin realized Teddy was right. The blonde was obviously there for someone in the band and the brunette was the fifth wheel regretting accompanying her now. It was a shame, really, practically a crime, *not* to be having fun in New Orleans on Mardi Gras—especially since she'd obviously come for the celebrations, not to listen to some just-shy-of-crappy band. "How long is their set?"

Teddy sighed. "They're booked for two."

He nearly choked. "Really? They're not that good."

"Tell me something I don't know. But every decent band in the parish was booked."

Two hours into the first of two three-hour sets. The poor girl had a long day ahead of her if the blonde truly was there as the band's groupie.

And her phone's battery was bound to go dead eventually.

"You should go talk to her."

Sleep deprivation was definitely doing damage to Teddy's brain. "What?"

"I feel bad for her. Plus, she's kinda bad for business, sitting there like that all miserable. People can see her from the street and they'll think twice about coming in here." Teddy grinned. "Consider it a favor."

"I'm barely done with the last favor and you're asking for another?"

Teddy grinned. "If I recall correctly, your exact words were, 'I'll owe you for life.'"

Damn it. Five years ago, the money Teddy had invested had been the final and crucial piece launching *No Quarter* and Rainstorm Games into the big leagues. He and Eric had pulled together every last cent they'd had—forgoing all but the most basic of human survival requirements—and had come up short. Teddy hadn't had the money to spare at the time, but he'd given it anyway, pulling the cash out of his own business savings to support theirs.

Colin had meant the sentiment at the time, but he'd never thought he'd regret it. And it wasn't as if Teddy regretted the money; the return on that investment had allowed him to open the Lucky Gator three years earlier than anyone expected. "Seriously, now, how long do you think you can keep playing that card?"

"The rest of your life, my friend. The rest of your life." Slapping Colin's shoulder, Teddy went behind the bar. "What? You got big plans or something?"

"Maybe," he hedged.

"Plans *other* than locking yourself in your office and working?" Teddy grinned, knowing he'd gotten it right. As if Teddy had room to talk. He, Eric, Colin…they were all practically workaholics. Growing up just shy of poor and building your business from scratch often did that to people.

"Come on," Teddy coaxed. "There's a damsel in distress over there, Lancelot, so go save her. You know you want to."

Actually, he didn't. He'd done nothing but put out fires all day, and he was done with the whole thing. But... she did look miserable. "Fine. But we're going to have a discussion about hyperbole and the shelf life of favors owed after this."

Colin grabbed a bottle of water and went over. "Something wrong with your beer?" He practically had to shout over the music, but she did hear him.

The brunette looked up, startled at the interruption. Her eyes were a deep, deep green, and tiny freckles dotted her cheekbones. Strands of dark hair had escaped her braid to coil around her temples from the humidity. Close up, she was an all-American, fresh-faced, girl-next-door beauty. "Excuse me?"

"Your beer. You're not drinking it. Something wrong with it?"

Her eyebrows pulled together briefly in confusion, then she seemed to notice the Lucky Gator logo on his T-shirt, and she smiled as she shook her head. "No, it's fine. Just a little early in the day for me to be drinking."

"That sentiment rather puts you in the minority today."

A small smile tugged at her lips. "Indeed. But I've got all day, so I need to pace myself."

He held up his water bottle. "Right there with you. Do you mind if I take this chair?"

"Oh, sure. Go ahead. We're not using it."

At her look of surprise when he sat down, Colin realized she'd thought he meant to take the chair away, not join her. He bit back a smile and stuck his hand out. "Colin."

She shook it. "Jamie." There was something careful about the way she said it, and her posture changed to be more guarded.

He pointed toward the bar. "That's Teddy. He owns the Lucky Gator."

Jamie followed his finger, and Teddy waved at her. With a small, slightly confused smile, she waved back.

"Teddy is concerned that you're not having a very good time in his establishment."

An eyebrow went up. "So you've been sent over here to find out why?"

She was honest, it seemed. No false assertions or denials. "Something like that. He seems to think I might be able to entertain you a little, since the music isn't doing it." He leaned forward. "Not that I blame you for having better taste than that."

"That's very kind of you and Teddy both, but I'm sure you're very busy today and have better things to do than entertain me."

"Teddy is busy. I'm done, thank God."

Jamie's head cocked sideways, causing the end of her braid to fall over her shoulder and into the cleavage that peeked through the colorful beads. "Your shift is over already? I'd think the big money would be made later today."

It took him a second to catch up. Jamie assumed he was Teddy's employee, which, considering the circumstances, wasn't a bad guess. But he didn't feel the need to correct her, either. The truth would require explanations and this really wasn't the time for that. "This place will be a zoo in a few more hours. And once the parades are over, it will be a complete madhouse. There's not enough money on the planet to get me to work that shift." *And Teddy knows not to even try to call in that as a favor.*

"It gets that crazy, huh?"

He laughed. "This must be your first Mardi Gras."

Jamie's nose crinkled. "Is it that obvious?"

"Pretty much. The big giveaway is that you're sitting here *not* having a good time when no matter what your definition of a good time is, it can be found right beyond those doors."

She sighed wistfully. "Yeah, this was not what I expected to do today, but I came with Kelsey and she wants to listen to David play."

"Boyfriend?"

"Not yet, but she's hopeful about it. And since I don't know my way around or anything, I'm stuck here with her."

"What did you want to do today?" There was literally something for everyone, but since she'd already ruled out drinking, she obviously had something else in mind.

She smiled and it lit up her face. "I wanted to see the parades, of course. We caught a little bit of Zulu on the way in, but we were carrying the band's stuff and couldn't hang out to really watch."

He looked at the clock over the bar. "Rex should be getting to Canal shortly. The truck parades follow it. There's still plenty of parade goodness available, if that's what you want."

He could tell she wanted to, but that she was tamping down the desire. "Yeah, but I don't think Kelsey's really interested."

"Go without her."

She wrinkled her nose. It was kind of adorable. *She* was kind of adorable. "It wouldn't be much fun to go alone."

"It couldn't be less fun than you're having now."

"True." She fiddled with the beads around her neck, seemingly torn. "But would it be safe to go by myself? This may be my first Mardi Gras, but I have heard stories and I'm not stupid."

That did show good sense. "Well, you're sober, so that increases your safety exponentially right there. And you'd only need to go about two or three blocks on well-populated streets in the middle of the day, so I think you'd be all right. There's a lot of people, but there's also a lot of police around. If it was dark and you were planning on wandering the Quarter alone, I'd say differently."

"I don't know." He could hear the indecision in her voice, the desire to go somewhere else battling with the common sense not to wander about alone in a strange city. "When I was a teenager, my mother used to tell me that it wasn't me she didn't trust, it was the situation." Her mouth twisted into a wry smile. "And if there was ever an untrustworthy situation, this would probably be it."

"Want me to go with you?" It wasn't until Jamie's eyebrows disappeared into her hairline in shock that he realized what he'd said. The offer had just come out of nowhere, without forethought, and he was almost as shocked as Jamie that he'd even made it. But he couldn't just let her sit here when it was such an easy thing to fix.

Jamie was quick to recover, though. "That's very kind of you, but I'm sure you have other plans today."

He realized that was almost as suave of an invitation as she could get from any number of random dudes on the street. She'd just said she wasn't stupid, and her refusal—as polite as it was—showed it.

But he was oddly disappointed. He'd known her for all of five minutes—and without Teddy's intervention he wouldn't have known her at all—but being shot down like that still stung, no matter how much sense it made. And it wasn't as if it would help to mention that she'd be perfectly safe with him; he was pretty sure most serial killers professed what nice guys they were, too.

"I have no other plans," *that much was almost true*

"and I'd be happy to go with you for a while and walk you back here when you've seen enough."

He could tell Jamie was really tempted. She was clearly bored out of her mind here and desperate to do something else, but he understood her hesitation at wandering off with a guy she'd just met. He'd kill his sister if she ever did exactly what he was suggesting to Jamie. At the same time, he was growing more and more interested in her and actually wanted her to accept his offer.

Then the band hit a particularly discordant note, and Jamie winced. That seemed to shake her out of her indecision. She tapped her friend on the shoulder. "Kelsey, give me your phone."

The blonde turned around for the first time. "What? Why?" she asked as she handed it over.

Jamie held it up in his direction. "Smile."

Caught off guard, he did, and Jamie took his picture.

"Kelsey, this is Colin. He's a bartender here." Jamie was typing into the phone as she spoke, but Kelsey sized him up and smiled at him appreciatively. Then Jamie looked at him again. "Last name?"

This didn't make a lot of sense, but he answered anyway. "Raine."

"R-A-I-N?"

"E," he added automatically.

"Thanks." She handed the phone back to her friend. "Colin and I are going up to Canal to watch the parade."

Kelsey gave Jamie a look and a smirk. "Really, now? How interesting." The innuendo in her voice all but had them doing it in an alley fifteen minutes from now.

Jamie frowned back at her. "I'll meet you back here later. I've got my phone with me, so send me a text if you go somewhere else."

Kelsey gave Jamie a big smile and then winked at him

suggestively. He wasn't unaccustomed to having women flirt with him, but that wink bordered on tawdry and made him feel a little dirty. "Y'all have fun."

Jamie stood. Until now, he'd only seen her from the waist up, but that white T-shirt tucked into a pair of cut-offs exposing tanned legs and firm thighs. She wasn't tall, maybe only chin height on him, but everything was perfectly proportioned.

So far he had no real reason to regret his impromptu and unexpected invitation.

Then Jamie grinned at him, her excitement clearly evident and surprisingly contagious to someone who should have been long immune to the parades. "Let's go."

Chartres Street wasn't completely packed, but it was busy, requiring Jamie to stay close as he helped guide her through the throng. "What was that about?" he asked.

She turned to look at him, mild confusion wrinkling her forehead. "What was what about?"

"The phone. The photo."

"Oh." She shrugged. "Just in case I go missing, Kelsey has your photo and name to give to the police," she answered matter-of-factly. "This may not be the smartest thing I've ever done, but I don't have to be completely stupid about it either."

Bold but cautious. Funny and smart. He put a hand on her back as he shouldered through a group gathered under a balcony begging beads from the people above.

Nope, no regrets at all.

I, Jamie Vincent, am a complete idiot. Her biography, if it were ever written, would carry the title *But It Seemed Like a Good Idea at the Time.*

She was alone, in a still-strange city, during one of

the biggest street parties in the world, with a man she'd met ten minutes ago as her only guide.

But Colin didn't seem creepy or shady—he hadn't triggered any of her internal alarms—and it was broad daylight. She was sober, he was sober and there were, quite literally, thousands of people and police around. Surely it was safe enough to just watch a parade. Hell, Kelsey was so infatuated with David, she wasn't exactly holding up her end of the buddy system anyway.

She couldn't even get angry about it, either. Kelsey was just someone who'd agreed to rent her a room when she answered Kelsey's ad. They weren't exactly besties or anything. Kelsey didn't owe her a good time, because Jamie was technically infringing on her Mardi Gras celebration to start with.

If I end up dead in a Dumpster, I'll have only myself to blame.

She had a basic map of New Orleans in her head, but she'd only been here two whole days—and she'd spent most of that just trying to get settled in—so it was patchy at best. Chartres would cross Canal and become Camp, and Camp would get her home. That much she knew. As long as she stayed on the main streets, she shouldn't get too lost or turned around.

The crowds got thicker as they approached Canal, and she found herself pressed closer to Colin. That wasn't exactly a bad thing, she admitted to herself. Amid the general smell of stale beer and teeming masses of people, Colin smelled nice—like clean laundry. Plus, Colin had a rather nice body to be pressed against—athletic, but not muscle-bound. A girl could do much worse.

"Here, hold my hand."

The instruction startled her, and she looked up at him. Colin grinned as he held out his hand. He had a great smile that caused little crinkles at the corners of bright blue eyes. A shock of dark hair—just long enough to curl around his ears, as if he was a few weeks late for a haircut—was held back from his face by the sunglasses perched on his head.

Goodness, he was just damn pretty.

But that didn't mean she was going to hold hands.

The sentiment must have showed on her face, because Colin laughed as he cocked an eyebrow at her. "I'm not trying to get fresh. I just don't want to lose you in the crowd."

It was a fair enough statement, but before she could reply, he flashed her another lady-killer grin. "Either that, or you could just stick your hands in my back pockets."

Without thinking, her eyes flicked down to the pockets in question, and *damn,* did he have to have a cute butt, too? *That* was tempting. *Way* too tempting.

For safety's sake, his first idea was probably the best one.

Jamie put her hand in his and Colin's fingers threaded through hers, bringing them palm to palm. His hands were warm, the grip firm but not painful, and there was one brief ridiculous moment where she was sure her skin tingled like the heroine's in some romance novel.

She almost wished he *would* get fresh.

No!

But he's so cute.

Down, girl. Have we learned nothing?

She had. And the lesson had been painful enough to ensure she wouldn't forget it.

She continued to tell herself that as she was hauled up against Colin's side, their clasped hands pressed against his chest as he maneuvered through the crowd. Jamie just did her best to keep up.

Colin finally stopped near a streetlamp. "This should be good. Rex will come this way, but the trucks turn the other way up Canal, so to see them, you'll have to go up a few blocks."

Although crowds lined the barriers on both sides of the street, there was no sign of a parade. "So where is it?"

"Ah, timing can be a tricky thing. You never really know how long it will take for the parade to get to a specific spot. There are delays, the floats break down, you name it. But this—" he gestured to the crowd around them "—is part of the experience, too."

"So we wait?"

"We wait. Do you want a drink or anything?" When she shook her head, Colin sat and leaned back against the lamppost.

Although there was no telling how nasty the sidewalk might be, Jamie sat as well. She felt a little awkward now, this good idea faltering a bit as she tried to decide how to make small talk with a stranger—regardless of how pretty he might be. One thing she'd never been very good at was cocktail party chitchat.

Thankfully, though, Colin didn't seem to have the same problem. "Is this your first time in New Orleans?"

"No." She'd been down here a few years ago with Joey for a game before he'd moved up to the majors. Before everything had gotten crazy and gone to hell. But there was no way she was going to mention that. "It was a very short trip, though, on business with my boyfriend, so I didn't have much time to explore."

That eyebrow went up again. "Boyfriend?"

"Ex," she clarified.

Colin winked at her. "That's good to know."

Was that flirting or just charm? It was so hard to tell. She'd been out of the game for so long she didn't remember how to play. And she certainly didn't know how to respond. Joey had been the jealous type—possessive, actually, she amended with hindsight—so her flirting skills were rusty from disuse. Maybe she should delay even easing back into this.

Colin stretched long, tanned legs out and got comfortable. "So, where's home?"

Oh, it was going to be tough, though.

"South Carolina," she answered automatically, dragging her attention from those nice calf muscles. As he nodded, she realized that she'd just led Colin to believe that she was only in New Orleans for a short visit. Still, the statement wasn't entirely false. South Carolina *was* home, even if she didn't live there anymore and hadn't for a while. She'd followed Joey to five different cities and they'd never felt like home, and while she was here *now,* New Orleans didn't feel like home yet, either. So it wasn't entirely a false statement, and considering the circumstances, it probably wasn't a bad thing to let Colin keep that misunderstanding for now. She didn't trust herself not to flirt herself right into trouble accidentally. And since he could be an ax murderer for all she really knew, some vagueness about her living situation was probably wise. "And you?"

"Born and raised right here in New Orleans."

"A real ragin' Cajun, huh?"

His mouth twisted as if something was funny. "Something like that."

Oh, she just needed to slap a warning label right across his forehead. A good-looking, charming, self-professed ragin' Cajun bartender who just happened to have no plans on Fat Tuesday other than to escort a woman around... Oh, the dangers were piling up, and Jamie knew she should just cut and run. But, *oh*... She could feel her libido crank its engine. Talk about her own personal Kryptonite. It was what had attracted her to Joey in the first place—a slightly rough-around-the-edges underdog with a big dream and charm to spare.

Really? This is how you're going to start out?

It had been her downfall before; it would be stupid to repeat the experience.

But maybe just for today?

How much trouble could she get into, really? It wouldn't be anything serious, just one day to enjoy herself before the new life kicked in. It made sense—Mardi Gras was *supposed* to be the big decadent party before the austerity of Lent. One last day before life got real again. Hell, she couldn't even assume he'd stick around longer than this parade anyway. They were talking about an hour or so, max. What harm could really come of it?

It was a beautiful day, sunny and warm, she had a cute, seemingly nice enough guy to talk to, and she was in the middle of a crowd that just wanted to have a good time. She felt free, powerful, in charge of her own life again.

She really couldn't ask for more, could she?

She deserved a break. After everything she'd dealt with—the pain, the shame, the complete destruction of her life—she'd earned this Fat Tuesday and all the decadent fun it could bring her.

She could have today, by God.

The noise level had been increasing steadily, and now music floated over the top of the roar. It kept her from having to respond.

Colin pushed to his feet. "Here it comes." He extended a hand to help her up. She was still justifying everything to herself as Colin hauled her up and stationed himself behind her as the crowd pushed forward toward the street and the barricades.

His chest was broad and hard against her back, and one hand came to rest easily and naturally on her hip as he leaned forward to tell her something. He was wearing shorts, like she was, and she could feel the hair on his legs tickling her calves and thighs. She totally missed whatever it was he was trying to say.

"What?"

"Don't reach down if anything hits the ground. You'll get your hands stomped."

What the hell were they throwing off these floats? Diamonds? She twisted around to look at him. "Over cheap plastic beads?"

"Yep."

"Seriously?"

Colin laughed, patting her hip as he did. It left a nice residual tingle. "Oh, honey, you have no idea. Look, there's Rex."

Jamie strained up on tiptoe, craning her neck to see. *Wow.* She'd heard these parades were amazing, and she'd expected something really cool, but this…. A massive gilded throne, ornate costumes with feathers and men on horseback in matching courtier outfits with satin pantaloons…just *wow.*

She jumped up and down to get a better view, accidentally bumping against Colin's chin in the process.

"Can you not see?" he asked. She shook her head and tried to use his shoulder as a boost when she jumped this time. A second later, she felt hands on her legs and the whisper of hair against her thighs. She jumped for real this time.

Colin was crouched behind her. "Come on. Climb up."

He didn't wait for an answer, and she felt the broad base of his shoulders pressing against the backs of her thighs as Colin's head dipped between her knees. Then she was up over the crowd—with an amazing view of the parade—with Colin holding her as though she weighed nothing at all. He shrugged to get her settled, and she quickly wrapped her legs behind his back to anchor herself.

"Better?" he shouted up.

She was still reeling from the fact his head was now between her *thighs* and a rather personal bit of her anatomy was now pressed against the nape of his neck. Funny how she'd never noticed the inappropriateness of this position until just now. "Yeah," she answered, but it sounded a little weak even to her own ears. "Are you sure I'm not too heavy?"

"Oh, please. I can barely tell you're up there."

"Now what do I do?"

Colin tilted his head way back, nearly sending her toppling over before she corrected by leaning forward, and grinned at her again. "Catch whatever comes your way. And no matter what you've seen on TV, don't flash the riders for beads," he cautioned. "You'll get us both arrested."

"*Flash* them—?" she began, but she was cut off when something hit her right in the face.

She caught it reflexively and a strand of green-and-gold beads dangled from her fingers.

"Good job," Colin said, patting her knee. "Now put them on." She looped them over her head as a shower of beads began to rain down from the floats.

Colin caught a few, but for the most part, he kept his arms locked around her legs to keep her stable as she quickly got the hang of it. Occasionally, she'd loop a set over his head until he began to look a bit like a cheap Technicolor Mr. T.

There were marching bands, more elaborate costumes, ornate floats—just an ongoing stream of tacky, over-the-top opulence. And Jamie loved every minute of it. She'd had no idea she was such a sucker for a parade, and the crowd's enthusiasm was contagious. This was *so* much better than sitting at the Lucky Gator listening to a crappy band play, and she finally understood the allure of the street party.

This was simply freakin' *awesome*.

Colin kept pointing out details and providing back-story, acting as her own private Mardi Gras guide and tutor. When a float broke down, bringing the parade to a halt, Colin got her a beer from a street vendor and then danced with her to a high school marching band's rendition of "Louie, Louie" before putting her back on his shoulders for the last few floats. She was sad to see the final one go by.

As the crowd began to pull back a little, Colin set her on her feet for the last time.

Rising up onto her tiptoes again, she kissed his cheek, surprising them both. "That was *so* much fun. Thank you."

"My pleasure. Want me to walk you back to the bar?"

Jamie fished her phone out of her pocket. No message from Kelsey, so she was probably still there listening to David's band mangle another classic, and she didn't really want to go back now, anyway.

Colin must have picked up on her mood. "*Or* we could head a couple of blocks up the street and watch the next one?"

A happy glow settled in her stomach. "I think I'd like that. A lot, actually."

To her surprise, he seemed genuinely pleased with her answer. He held out his hand. "Then let's go."

This time, she didn't think twice about taking it.

Let the good times roll.

CHAPTER TWO

THEY ATE MUFFULETTAS bought from a food cart near Woldenberg Park as the sun went down. Jamie didn't really care for the olives, but she wasn't complaining. About anything.

Today hadn't been what she'd expected—who *could* have expected this?—and if anyone had tried to tell her she'd have one of the best days of her life at a street party with a guy she barely knew, she'd have laughed in their face.

Colin wadded up the wrapper from his sandwich and tossed it into an already overflowing garbage can. New Orleans was a beautiful place, but it was definitely worse for wear today, with garbage littering the streets and a pervasive odor of stale beer, sweat and something else she didn't even want to try to identify. She could relate, though. Like the city, she wasn't exactly fresh as a daisy now either, but she was still thrumming with energy and excitement and the desire for a good time.

She might just come to love New Orleans.

That might not be a good thing.

"Your nose is turning pink," Colin said.

Jamie wrinkled it experimentally and felt the tightness. "Great. I'm going to have a clown nose."

"Cutest clown ever." He reached out a finger and

touched it gently, his eyebrows drawing together in concern. "Does it hurt?"

The proximity, the gentle touch, the concern in his voice…Jamie's throat felt tight and that tingly anticipation slid up through her stomach again. "No. Not yet," she managed to get out.

He nodded and traced a finger along her cheekbone. "You're a little pink here, too."

Colin was killing her. There'd been flirting all day, the friendly, teasing kind that danced along the line but never went over it, leaving her wondering if it was just his personality or genuinely directed at her. She'd scraped the rust off her own flirting skills and given it her best, but the results were unsatisfying—in multiple ways. She had no idea if she was having any effect on him at all, and if not, was it from lack of interest on his part or lack of skill on hers?

She'd been touching him for hours—even once wrapping her arms around his waist and pressing against his back as they went through a particularly dense crowd—but she wanted to *really* touch him. She'd found herself staring at his lips, her mouth gone dry and her stomach fluttering, but Colin never made the move. Even when he touched her—a hand on her back to guide her, holding her hand in the crowd, even once wrapping an arm around her shoulders and pulling her in close and protectively when a couple of drunk guys got a little too rowdy—it hadn't been more than what she'd expect from any male friend. It bordered on brotherly, for God's sake.

And it was completely, absolutely *killing* her.

Surely Colin wouldn't spend this much time with a woman he didn't feel *some* attraction to? This might have started out as a step above a pity date, but he could have gone his own way at any time. The fact that he hadn't gave her hope.

If this was some kind of game, he was playing her like a pro, but it didn't *feel* like a game, and that both pleased and concerned her. Because if she was being played, she was falling for it, hook, line and sinker, and she couldn't stop herself if she wanted to. And she wasn't sure she really wanted to anyway.

But if Colin didn't make a move on her soon, she was going to launch herself at him like a penis-seeking missile, probably humiliating them both at the same time.

She drained the last of her beer, wishing she had a few more in her system—just enough to cause her to lose the inhibition that kept her from acting on the ideas running wild and free through her mind.

But *no,* she'd just had to be somewhat responsible today.

Just enjoy this for what it is. Don't ruin it by making a complete fool of yourself.

She was probably misreading the situation anyway. Maybe this was just some New Orleans tradition she was unaware of—a local interpretation of Southern hospitality: find a bored tourist and show her a good time.

And hadn't she proven—conclusively—that she was really bad at reading people, unable to even pick up on the glaringly obvious, much less the subtle? She wouldn't even be here if she had the ability to judge people correctly. At the same time, she was still glad she was.

So this was a nightmare—an oddly pleasant and exciting nightmare, but a nightmare nonetheless.

Colin's finger moved away. "Yep, definitely a few new freckles, too."

Sweet mercy. She was in such a mind-versus-libido turmoil time was practically standing still while it was grinding away. Not that those frozen moments in time were necessarily a bad thing…

She took a deep breath, but Colin's phone rang before she could say anything. He took it out, glanced at the screen and sent the call to voice mail, but not before she had the chance to see the smiling face of a *very* attractive woman on the screen. "Feel free to answer that," she said as casually as possible.

He shook his head. "It's just Elise. One of our friends is having a party today, and she probably just wants to know where I am."

"Oh." She forced herself to smile instead of asking who Elise was.

As if he could read her mind, Colin offered, "Elise is my baby sister, by the way."

She had to fight not to show relief in that news. "Well, if you need to go, then don't let me keep you." She tried to sound casual about it. "You've been great to show me around, and it's been really fun." She fished her own phone out and checked Kelsey's last message. "Kelsey and David are barhopping, and I can go catch up with them."

Colin lifted an eyebrow at her. "I'll take you back to your friends now, if that's what you want."

"God, no." Jamie stopped and cleared her throat. She toyed with her watch, trying to look nonchalant. "I mean, I'm having a good time with you, but I really do understand if you want to…"

He leaned back on his elbows in the grass and crossed his feet at the ankles. "Do I look like someone who's in a hurry to go somewhere else?"

She felt herself smile and just hoped it wasn't too goofy-looking. "I guess not."

Colin rolled slightly toward her. "So what *do* you want to do now?"

A dozen images jumped immediately to mind, and she gritted her teeth to keep from describing them in detail. "I guess we could go back to the Quarter? After all you've said about it, I'm kinda curious to see the insanity for myself."

He looked doubtful. "Are you sure?"

No, but you're not giving me better options. "Isn't it part of the full Mardi Gras experience?"

"Oh, honey, it's an experience all its own." He leaned all the way back, stacking his hands behind his head. Turning his head toward her, he arched an eyebrow. "You think you can handle it?"

That was a tad insulting. "Of course I can handle it. Why would you think I couldn't?"

"It's way outside your comfort zone."

"You know nothing about my comfort zone," she protested.

"You blushed when that drunk guy propositioned you, and he wasn't even that graphic about it."

That was true, but the blush hadn't come from the guy's proposition. She'd been hoping *Colin* would make her that offer, and that was what had made her blush. "It simply caught me off guard." She tried to add an airy wave, but accidentally caught one of the many, many beads around her neck in the clasp of her watch instead, and had to take a moment to untangle herself.

"There will be nudity, adult situations, suggestive language…"

"So it's an X-rated event," she interrupted. "I'm a grown woman and this is the internet age, you know. I don't think I'm that shockable."

That earned her a smile. "Then let's do it." He rolled

to his feet and brushed the grass off before extending a hand to help her up. The crowds weren't quite as thick here, so Colin didn't take her hand—sadly—but he did put his hand on the small of her back again to guide her. She was so primed, even that simple touch was downright torture.

The wind off the river blew the hair that had escaped her braid into her eyes as they walked, but the breeze felt good.

She'd chosen New Orleans as her new hometown almost on a whim. It was far enough away to be a fresh start, but it also seemed like the kind of vibrant, exciting place where a person could truly reinvent herself. And after a few Midwest winters, the climate seemed ideal.

She hadn't had time yet to explore the city, but she was now making a mental list of all the places she wanted to explore sooner rather than later. As they turned toward Jackson Square, all lit up with the cathedral behind it, she began to fall in love. "I can't wait to see what New Orleans is like when it's not Mardi Gras."

"There's always something going on," Colin said, "but it's not always crazy like this. It's a good bit cleaner, too," he added, kicking a plastic cup into the gutter with the other trash.

"You really love this city, don't you?" He'd been a walking, talking guidebook all day, and she belatedly realized that it was genuine love and pride for his hometown causing it—not just the need to inform or impress with his knowledge.

"What's not to love?" he asked, spreading his arms wide to embrace the city. Directly to his left, a college-age girl was loudly being sick into a garbage can. "Well, except for that," he corrected and steered her away.

The crowds were getting thicker and Colin reached

for her hand as they moved farther into the Quarter. This time, though, he pulled her in front of him, letting his arm cross her chest like a seat belt, pressing her against his chest and tucking a hand into the back waistband of her shorts. "Whatever you do, don't let go of me. I'll never find you in this crowd."

Jamie just wanted to lean against him for awhile—maybe rub a little against that chest—but Colin was pushing her forward into the mass of people on St. Peter's Street. She didn't think it would be possible, but the crowd got even denser as they crossed Royal, edging closer to Bourbon Street and the epicenter of all things.

Oh, the internet had not prepared her for *this*. She'd been expecting costumes, and she wasn't disappointed. Most of them weren't as elaborate as those worn in the parades, but some did try with large amounts of feathers and rhinestones. The closer they got to Bourbon, however, the smaller the costumes got—leaving elaborate behind in favor of exposure.

There was a man wearing nothing more than a strategically placed jester's hat and harlequin face paint walking with a man in a crown and a cape who displayed a very long…um…*scepter*. A man on stilts wearing lingerie and a feathered mask. And the women—she'd never seen so many breasts before, either exposed as a part of the costume or simply bared in order to be showered with beads. Every body shape and type was on display, and she had to have a bit of respect for the people with enough self-confidence to let it all hang out like that—literally.

Jamie hadn't led a sheltered life, but she had lived a rather circumspect one. She'd been a good girl from a nice middle-class family; there simply hadn't been much trouble for her to get in to. She'd flirted with rebellion in college, but then she'd met Joey, who had always worked so hard to keep his public image squeaky clean, to be the kind of player that kids would look up to and their parents would be glad for it. It had been one of the things she'd loved about him—even if she now knew it was all a lie—and she'd been happy to adjust her expectations accordingly. So while Joey had been doing a lot of wild partying—along with other things—behind her back, she'd never been a part of that lifestyle. Now her eyes felt as if they were bugging out of her head.

She heard Colin chuckle in her ear. "I tried to warn you."

"I'm amazed, but you can hold off on the smelling salts." She twisted around to look at him. "This is unbelievable, though. Is it legal to get naked like that?"

Colin shrugged. "Public nudity is illegal, but on Bourbon Street—especially this time of year—as long as you're not causing a ruckus, you're probably safe from arrest."

"I guess the police have plenty of bigger fish to fry today."

"Exactly."

Their progress through the crowd had been slow but steady, giving Jamie the opportunity to look around and absorb all she could, but then they got caught in a raucous pack parked under a balcony.

She'd seen women flashing their breasts from the balconies above and expected this to be more of the same. But she looked up to see a couple embracing quite passionately for their audience. The man had his hand under the woman's shirt and her leg was hooked around his waist. When the people below began shouting both encouragement and suggestions, the couple began to incorporate the suggestions into their tableau.

Jamie felt her jaw go slack. While she'd never been

much of a voyeur before, it was somehow impossible *not* to watch. It was simultaneously tawdry and erotic, and in this sexually charged atmosphere, its effect on the crowd was electric.

And Jamie wasn't immune to the effect. She found herself leaning back into Colin a little too much, craving his smell and his heat. She couldn't help herself.

Colin wasn't unaffected by this either, and the fingers that held her waistband seemed to move gently against her back like a caress. Colin's fingers tightened around hers. She returned the squeeze.

Her knees went a little weak and she sagged against him as he exhaled near her ear, and the warmth of his breath caused gooseflesh to rise on her neck.

The noise and the lights and the crowd surrounding her seemed to disappear as Colin's thumb traced circles against her palm. Her free hand came to rest on the outside of his thigh, and she felt the muscles under the fabric tighten.

Then the crowd moved, sending the guy in front of her staggering backward to bump into her. Drunk and rowdy, he took it as an introduction and made a descriptive suggestion to *her*.

Before she could do more than gasp, Colin had released her hand and pushed the guy back with a very succinct suggestion of his own. And while her erstwhile admirer was fueled by testosterone and copious amounts of alcohol, Colin stood a full head taller and several inches wider. The man's friends wisely pulled him back.

Colin shoved the rest of the way through the crowd and back into the street, where the people were at least moving. "Sorry about that. You okay?"

"Yeah." Although he'd pulled her back against him, the moment had been ruined, and Jamie felt her cheeks

burning. She'd been caught in a slow simmer all afternoon, but the overcharged, overindulged raunchiness
around her made that moment under the balcony feel
slightly tawdry now. She wanted out of the Quarter and
back to the earlier mood. "I think I've seen—"

She gasped as a blonde in a very small tank top stum-
bled over her own feet and the drink in her hand landed
all over Jamie. Something slushy and pink covered most
of her shoulders and chest, and icy rivulets slid down her
cleavage. Against the heat and humidity, the cold and wet
drink initially felt refreshing, but Jamie's eyes watered
from the alcohol fumes even as it soaked through her
shirt and bra to her skin, replacing that refreshing feeling with clammy stickiness.

The girl mumbled an apology, but she seemed more
upset by the loss of her drink than the fact that Jamie
was now wearing it. The way the girl was weaving, the
loss of alcohol was probably a blessing, although Jamie
didn't doubt she'd get a refill quickly enough.

Colin took a look at her and shook his head. "Have
you had enough of the Quarter now?"

Wet, sticky and still reeling from that earlier moment,
she gritted out, "Very much so."

Colin surveyed the damage. "Come on. Let's go get
you cleaned up."

That didn't seem likely or even possible, and there was
something slightly humiliating about the whole thing,
but she was now miserable in more ways than she could
count, and getting off Bourbon Street seemed like a very
good idea regardless. She let Colin lead her through a less
crowded back alley she'd never walk into alone, not even
for money, and when they emerged on Chartres Street,
she realized they were going back to the Lucky Gator.

She'd come full circle.

* * *

He shouldn't have brought Jamie back into the Quarter—
or at the very least, he should have kept her off Bourbon Street. He certainly knew better, even if she didn't.
It was too out of control, with too many people acting
like idiots and bordering on dangerous. But there was
something about Jamie that made him want to indulge
her. She seemed to want to experience everything, give
it all at least one try, and she embraced everything with
enthusiasm and excitement.

And he had to admit he was rather hoping she'd indulge him back—hopefully with a bit of that enthusiasm, too. It was getting damn near impossible to keep
his hands to himself. What had started off as a lark, a
little good deed to show her a good time, had turned into
something else. Sure, Jamie was gorgeous and he wasn't
immune to that, but there was also something…*refreshing* about her as well. Something wholesome and sweet
that stood out against the decadence of Mardi Gras and
made him see the event through new eyes.

But playing tour guide today of all days had brought
its own issues. He'd had her pressed against him so many
times today, felt the soft skin of her inner thigh against
his cheek…. All perfectly innocent and understandable
in the situation, but what it was doing to him was far
from understandable *or* innocent.

And while part of him wanted to believe that Jamie
would want to cross that line, he wasn't entirely sure the
signals he was seeing weren't just figments of a hopeful
imagination. Hell, he was sorely tempted to press her up
against the alley wall and offer to lick every drop of that
drink off her skin.

Maybe Fat Tuesday wasn't the best day to meet someone new. At the same time, the clock was ticking. At best,

she might be in town only a day or two longer—he'd have to ask—and the knowledge of a deadline only made the need to touch her more acute.

The hand holding his was sticky, which was one of the main reasons he was taking her back to the Lucky Gator. They slipped in the back door, past a long line of people waiting for the restrooms, and stopped in front of a door marked Private.

"Just stay here for a second." Jamie looked bedraggled, but she nodded. It took a bit of time to make his way to the bar, where Teddy and his staff were moving at high speed to keep up with the crowd that now spilled out the doors into the street, and even longer to get Teddy's attention. "I need your office keys."

Either Teddy trusted him or was simply too busy to care, because he tossed the keys Colin's way without question or comment.

Jamie was where he left her, doing her best to brush the worst off, and she looked at him questioningly as he unlocked the door. "We can get you a dry shirt from Teddy's office." Looking her over, he saw the slush ran down her leg into her shoes. That wasn't going to be much fun to walk around in. "Not sure there's much we can do about the shoes, though."

"It's fine. I'm going to burn them tomorrow anyway."

At least this hadn't dampened her spirit.

The hallway was quieter as the door closed behind him, and he grabbed a couple of clean bar towels off the shelf. After wetting one in the mop sink, he handed both to her as he unlocked the office and led her inside. It was small and untidy, and Jamie looked uncomfortable being in there. "You can get the worst of it off with those, and I'll see about finding you a shirt."

"Thanks." Taking the wet cloth, she wiped it over her

arms and hands, then closed her eyes and sighed in pleasure as she wiped her face and the parts of her neck not
covered in beads. "Oh, that feels *so* good."

He swallowed hard as he watched her. Jesus, he really
was on edge, if that simple action was enough to send
his blood running south.

Shirt. Find her a clean shirt. He rummaged through
the boxes of Lucky Gator T-shirts under Teddy's desk
until he heard her curse quietly. Looking up, he saw her
fighting with the huge stack of beads around her neck.
"You okay?"

"I suddenly feel like I'm being strangled."

"Here. Let me help. Lean forward." She gave him
a look, but then did as he said. "All the way." He slid
his hands along the sides of her neck, under the plastic
strands and lifted them away from her skin. "Now just
drop your head forward…more. That's it. Now pull back."

The mass slipped onto his arms and Jamie stood up.
"Oh, my God. I feel ten pounds lighter all of a sudden."
She ran her hands over her neck and grinned. "Overac-
cessorizing is a bad thing."

He dropped the beads onto the desk and went back
to the box of T-shirts. "Let's get you a dry shirt. You'll
have to wear a gator across your chest."

"Thanks. This one is beyond help."

"It's probably going to be big on you…"

As he turned around, the rest of the sentence died in
his throat. Jamie was already matter-of-factly peeling her
shirt up, exposing a flat stomach and a bra so barely there
that he could see the dark shadows of her nipples through
the fabric. As the shirt cleared her head, she noticed him
staring. He expected her to cover herself, to turn around,
but instead, her movement slowed to a crawl. He looked

up, expecting to see shock, or even outrage, but her eyes met his evenly as her shirt hit the ground.

Just like that, the mood shifted, and the air felt close and tense. The noise just beyond the walls faded until Jamie's shallow breaths and the blood pounding in his ears blotted it out completely.

Unable not to, Colin let his fingers glide gently over the plane of her stomach, tracing the indentation that ran from ribs to navel, enjoying the little gasp and the way the muscles contracted under his touch. Jamie never broke the stare, even as he retraced his path up between her breasts, to the hollow at the base of her throat that fluttered under his fingers.

Jamie swallowed and her breath began to stutter. Her hand reached for the hem of his shirt, fisting in the fabric, pulling him closer to her until he could feel the heat from her skin. There was a moment where she seemed to inhale, her pupils dilating, and then Jamie rose to her tiptoes to press her mouth to his.

The sensation rocketed through him as if he'd been hit by lightning, causing his knees to buckle as he pulled her close and her tongue slid inside his mouth. He grabbed onto the filing cabinet with one hand and slid the other around the firm curve of her butt, steadying them both. Jamie moaned deep in her throat, and the sound nearly sent him over the edge right then.

Jamie's hands tangled in his hair, holding him when he moved to taste her neck, the skin on her collarbone, the soft spot behind her ear, and her leg rubbed restlessly against his.

He'd just wanted to touch her, nearly convincing himself that would be enough, but now… He wanted to explore her, devour her, lose himself in her.

The bra strap marred the smooth skin of her back,

but a quick twist of the clasp allowed him an unimpeded sweep from neck to waist. She dropped her arms, allowing it to fall the rest of the way to the floor, and leaned back against the door, giving him access to small, perfectly formed breasts. Jamie hissed as his thumb brushed over her nipple, and her whole body quivered.

She pushed his shirt up until it caught under his arms, and he let go of her long enough to remove his own beads and pull the shirt the rest of the way off. He tried to capture her lips again, but Jamie's head dipped to his chest, pressing hot kisses against his skin. He was having trouble breathing and then couldn't breathe at all when Jamie's tongue flicked over his nipple. He pressed his palms against the door hard, gritting his teeth as the pleasure seared through him.

Then she was kissing him again, hitching herself up to wrap her legs around his waist, her hips writhing against him. Any hope he had of rational thought or restraint was lost.

A tiny voice in the back of Jamie's mind was trying to send out a caution signal, but the rest of her was able to ignore it completely. She'd known she'd go right over if Colin so much as touched her, but she hadn't realized she could spontaneously combust in someone's arms or that it could feel *this* incredible when she did. It was better than her imaginings, more than her hopes. Colin was a freakin' gift from the sex gods, every inch of him designed to tempt and to please, and she didn't care if it was a good, bad or indifferent choice; she was going to take every bit she could and enjoy it.

Colin coaxed her legs back to the floor, then slid to his knees, hands grasping her hips as his mouth caught her nipple. The lights went dim as he sucked her, and without his support, she'd have collapsed altogether. Hot, wet kisses on the sensitive underside of her breast and across her ribs left her trembling. Then his tongue traced a path to her navel and beyond, inch by torturous inch until he finally reached the snap of her shorts.

He paused, his breath hot against her skin, and she looked down to see him watching her face, as though he was looking for permission to cross this last barrier. At the same time, his fingers were tracing along the hem of her shorts, teasing over her inner thighs, so close but yet so far from where she really needed them.

She reached for the snap and the zip, letting them sag from her hips. Colin surged back to his knees, his hand clasping her neck and pulling her down for a hot, wicked kiss at the same time his hand slid inside her panties.

Breaking the kiss, she gasped for air, holding onto his shoulders to steady herself. Colin's fingers circled and teased, wringing tiny moans from her. Just as she was about to scream in frustration, his hand twisted and his finger slipped inside her.

This time her knees did give out. Colin caught her in his lap, rolling to his back and then lowering her to the floor, never letting up on the sensations that had the edges of her mind fuzzy. She was panting, writhing, clawing at his back and the floor as he redoubled his efforts until she climaxed hard and fast.

She was vaguely aware of Colin reaching over her head, rummaging through desk drawers while she fumbled with the zipper of his shorts and palmed him. He stilled, his breath hissing out in pleasure, the muscles in his thighs shaking slightly as she worked her hand, trying to give him even half of what he'd given her. With a groan that sounded nearly painful, Colin grabbed her hand, planting a kiss in the palm and placing it on her stomach while he turned his attention back to the desk.

A second later, she heard a mumbled, "Thank God," and the distinctive sound of a foil packet being ripped open. Suddenly desperate, she shimmied her shorts down over her hips, letting Colin help push them to her ankles as he knelt between her thighs.

Dear God, he was absolutely gorgeous, eyes hooded and burning as he slid a hand from her pelvis to her neck, then met her eyes with a smile that was somewhere between pleased and predatory. It sent shivers of desire slicing though her, and she kissed him almost desperately as he slid slowly inside until their hips finally met. The sensation sent tiny shocks through her system, causing tremors she couldn't control. Bracing himself on his elbows, Colin held still as he kissed her, keeping the tremors going until Jamie began to buck and arch under him, demanding more. Slow and teasing quickly gave way to hot and frantic, and Jamie lost control, the intensity of it all both scary and exhilarating.

Jamie's breathing took almost a worrying amount of time to return to normal, but then, so did his. He'd come with a force that should have blown the top of his head off, so Colin was having a hard time gathering thoughts—any thoughts.

He heard Jamie sigh. He mustered enough strength to turn his head toward her and saw her staring at the ceiling. She sighed again. "Wow. That was…unexpected." A little smile tugged at her lips and she faced him. "Can I ask how you knew there'd be condoms in the desk?"

According to Teddy, one of the perks of owning a bar in the French Quarter was what happened after closing time. But he didn't really want to share that information with Jamie. "Um…"

She laughed. "On second thought, maybe I don't want to know."

He pushed up onto his elbow. "No, you really don't." Quite a bit more of her hair had come loose from her braid, and he toyed with a piece. Jamie leaned up and kissed him, a sweet, basking-in-afterglow kiss that had almost the opposite effect, reawakening his blood just when he thought he was half-dead.

He deepened the kiss even as the phone on Teddy's desk began to ring. It was annoying, but ignorable, even as the ancient answering machine picked up and the Lucky Gator's outgoing message played.

Teddy's voice was also the incoming message. The bar noise in the background was loud as Teddy shouted into the phone. "Dude, I don't know what you're doing in there, but I need change. I'm trying to run a business, for God's sake."

Jamie collapsed into giggles. "Busted." With a satisfied groan, she pushed to her elbows and sighed as she reached for her clothes. "Did you say something about a fresh shirt?"

Silently cursing Teddy—but applauding his timing nonetheless—he dropped a kiss on her bare shoulder. "Oh, yeah, *that's* why I brought you back here. I got a little sidetracked."

She took the shirt and slid it over her head. "Now we match."

"Consider it a Mardi Gras costume."

As he dressed, Jamie stuffed her ruined shirt and bra into the trash can and managed to untangle a few of her beads from the pile on the desk to put back around her neck. Holding the hopelessly tangled mound of remaining beads over the trash, she hesitated. "This seems wrong, somehow. I worked so hard to get them." With a shrug, she dropped them in.

Dressed now, Jamie tried to push the strands of hair that had fallen out of her braid back from her face. "I don't even want to know what I look like right now."

"You look amazing." Although Jamie rolled her eyes, as far as Colin was concerned, it was true. Her eyes were bright, cheeks pink and glowing, lips slightly swollen from his kisses. It was enough to make him decide to ignore Teddy's eviction attempt.

But even as he reached for her, Jamie had the door open and reality rushed right in.

"So what are we going to do now?" she asked.

Go back to my place? "Whatever you want."

"You know, I'm kinda feeling like I should give the French Quarter experience another try." She seemed to have a fresh burst of confidence—as well as a burst of energy he couldn't quite claim for himself.

"Are you sure?"

"Well, maybe we should start on Chartres and work our way back up to Bourbon Street."

It wasn't quite what he'd hoped to hear, but she wasn't heading back to her friends just yet and the night was still young.

This time Jamie followed him into the bar, only blushing slightly when Colin tossed the keys back to Teddy and Teddy gave her a knowing wink along with a couple of beers. "Great shirt. It looks much better on you than Colin. Y'all go have fun."

Jamie looked up at him and smiled. "I intend to."

CHAPTER THREE

OKAY, NOW SHE saw the attraction to the celebrations in the French Quarter. Maybe it was afterglow, maybe it was the fact that she wasn't so uncomfortably conscious of Colin now—although she was still very conscious of him, it was different now and definitely *not* uncomfortable—but regardless of why, Jamie was truly enjoying herself and exploring that bit of her that was just a little on the wild side. There was an anonymity to being in a crowd of strangers that downright *encouraged* her to explore it. Anonymity was something she hadn't had in a long time anyway, and it felt so damn good.

Colin's mood seemed to have shifted, too. More sure of her now, his charm was on full display, and he'd quit his best behavior, leaving her to discover he had a very wicked—and sometimes dirty—sense of humor. He'd kept it under wraps most of the day, making her question her initial judgment of his bad-boy tendencies, but they were there. Oh, yeah, they were there.

But she'd worry about all of that tomorrow. Tonight, she had a bit of a buzz going, a gorgeous man on her arm and absolutely no reason not to enjoy them both.

The entire Quarter was heaving with people, but she felt a part of the crowd, a part of the experience. She danced to the music that drifted out of the clubs and bars into the street, caught beads tossed from the balconies above, marveled at the costumes on display and in between enjoyed the feel of Colin's arms around her, the press of his body against hers and the occasional kiss he'd drop on her lips or neck.

It was the best night of her life and she was unwilling to let it end, even as Kelsey texted her repeatedly, wanting to go home now that she'd realized David wasn't all she'd hoped he'd be. She'd delayed and stalled until Kelsey had gone home without her, and now Jamie felt a bit bad. But Kelsey had ditched her first—figuratively, at least, by fawning over David—so Jamie didn't feel *really* bad about it for long.

Colin returned with their drinks and caught her frowning at her phone as she typed. "Everything okay?"

"Yeah." She hit send and stuffed the phone back in her pocket. "Kelsey's going home." She was pleased to see disappointment flash across Colin's face. "I told her I'd meet her there later."

Colin moved closer, a finger hooking in her pocket to tilt her hips toward his. "There's not a lot of later left of tonight."

She smiled up at him in what she hoped was a seductive manner. "Then I really need to enjoy what there is of it." *Now would be a good time for you to suggest we go back to your place, get a shower...* "What do you suggest—"

The question was interrupted by an earsplitting siren wail. She saw more than heard Colin curse as he grabbed her hand.

"What's going on?" she shouted, wanting to cover her ears as the siren wailed on and a surge of people pressed toward them.

"It's midnight. They're clearing the streets." Colin

pulled her against his chest as he tried to move sideways through the crowd toward the sidewalk. More sirens and honking horns joined the din, and her head began to throb from the noise. Jamie peeked over her shoulder to see a horizontal line of mounted police officers visible above the crowd and the strobe of red-and-blue police lights as they moved down Bourbon Street, instructing people by loudspeaker that Mardi Gras was over and they needed to clear the streets.

She was tripping over her own feet, being jostled from all sides, and only Colin's grip on her kept her from falling. The noise, the surge of people…it was the first time all evening that she'd felt scared, and she worried what would happen if she did fall. She gripped Colin's wrist with her free hand and trusted him to get them both through the melee.

At the corner—Jamie wasn't sure of which street— an influx of people caused a moment of gridlock. A girl bumped into her, and Jamie felt the heat of a lit cigarette against her arm. She jumped, trying to get away from the burn, and opened up a few inches of space between herself and Colin.

Those few inches, though, were all it took, as someone tried to move into the opening between them, forcing them farther apart. Colin's grip on her wrist tightened as he tried to shove the person out of the way and pull her back to him. Now she was trapped: a surge of cross traffic pulling her one way as Colin was pushed in the other direction, and the idiot who'd started it all was pressing against the arm Colin held, causing pain to shoot up from her elbow to her shoulder as though she was being stretched on the rack.

She could barely see Colin's head above the crowd. His lips were moving, but the sirens and crowd noise drowned the words out. Her grip on his wrist began to fail and while Colin's grip tightened more, pressing her watch painfully into her skin, his hand began to slip, too, until the connection was broken.

Jamie had no choice but to go with the flow. Her ears were ringing, her wrist was burning and her shoulder felt loose in the socket. Unable to see over the shoulders of those around her, she followed the crowd blindly, figuring eventually it would have to break. It was a slow-moving crowd, but a very thick one, and with all of her attention required to remain on her feet, she lost track of how long she'd been in the surge. There was a scuffle to her right and she caught an elbow in the head, causing her to see stars, and she began to panic a little.

The panic actually motivated her and she began to elbow her way out of the pack, finally reaching clear air and less congestion. Nothing looked familiar, and the street signs didn't help much beyond their distinctive style telling her she was still in the French Quarter.

There was no way in hell she was going back the way she came—even assuming it would be a straight shot back to familiar territory. About two blocks to her left, she could see a traffic light and figured that had to be Canal Street, so she headed that way.

Her head hurt, her ears were ringing, her heart was still pounding and her wrist was burning. She looked down to see that her watch was gone, the skin scratched and raw. It must have come off when Colin lost his grip.

Colin. She nearly turned around, but good sense prevailed. The exodus from the Quarter would be nearly impossible for her to fight against, and if the police were clearing the streets, did that mean she could get in trouble by going back in? She really didn't want to get arrested again.

Automatically, she reached for her phone, only to realize she'd never gotten his number. She hadn't needed to.

She could go back to the Lucky Gator; surely someone there would know how to get in touch with him...

What am I doing? It was bad enough she'd hooked up with Colin—who, now that she thought about it, she knew absolutely nothing about. She'd been enthralled and under his spell all day, but now that she was out of proximity, good sense came roaring back.

As if she didn't have *enough* going on right now. This was not how she needed to start off in a new city.

It had been a fun day, one for the memory books, but it was probably best it had ended like this. She should take it as a sign, an omen, that like all the other Mardi Gras celebrations, it had ended at midnight.

After all, the last thing she needed right now was to get involved with anyone. A new relationship of any sort had to be way down the priorities list, as she had to focus on the really important things right now.

So she should probably just go home.

Canal Street was a relief—still crowded, but the crowds were smaller and contained to the sidewalks. Without Colin's energy to feed from, weariness settled in on her quickly, and her feet began to drag. In front of a hotel, she stopped a cab driver who had just dropped off guests and begged for a ride home, offering triple the fare. When he finally agreed, she sank into the back seat with a sigh.

But what about Colin? He'd probably be worried about her, and she couldn't just let it end like that. As the cab crawled slowly through traffic, she looked up the phone number for the Lucky Gator on her phone.

The bar noise was so loud on the other end, the person who answered couldn't hear her, no matter how much she shouted—earning her sour looks from the cab driver. She tried three more times on the drive home, finally getting the answering machine on the fourth try. "I'm trying to get a message to Colin, um…" She searched her memory banks for his last name. *Sweet mercy, you had sex with the man and can't even remember his last name.* "Colin, the bartender. This is Jamie, and I just wanted him to know that I'm okay and made it home safely. I'll—" The machine beeped and cut her off.

She cursed, telling the machine exactly what it could do to itself in graphic terms, earning her another sour look from the driver. But he was easing to a stop in front of Kelsey's building, and Jamie figured that the signs were piling up, unable to be ignored. She paid the driver with the emergency fifty she'd stashed in her sock that morning and climbed the steps with heavy feet.

Only to find that her key had been lost somewhere in the Quarter, Kelsey wasn't answering the bell and her phone went immediately to voice mail. Near tears, Jamie sat on the stoop and dropped her head into her hands.

Oh, yeah. This had to be a sign.

Rainstorm Games had a carefully cultivated image as an exciting and dynamic company on the cutting edge of gaming. They had a wall full of awards celebrating their creativity and innovation, but on days like today, Colin missed those days when he and Eric had been holed up in that tiny hellhole of an apartment, building worlds for fun, but not necessarily profit.

Not that he didn't appreciate the profit—he did, very much so—and he was proud of the success they'd had, but some days were just frustrating.

Memory leaks were notoriously hard to find, but that didn't change the fact that they needed to find this one pretty damn quick. *Everyone* at Rainstorm—from him and Eric down to the newest intern—was going blind examining code. If they didn't release a patch soon, a horde of angry trolls—trolls *he'd* designed—was going to descend upon his office and feed him to the dragons as a sacrifice. This was not a problem he needed running up to the official launch, and the clock was ticking.

Frustrated, he took off his glasses and rubbed his eyes.

"Trouble in your post-apocalyptic dystopian zombie paradise?"

He looked up to see Callie in his doorway. "The zombies are fine. It's *Dungeons of Zhorg* that's glitching."

Callie shook her head in mock sympathy. "I just hate when that happens."

"So do several thousand users," he said, but Callie didn't take the hint, making herself comfortable on his couch instead. He knew her well enough to know that the quickest way to get her out of his office was to let her say whatever she'd come to say. "What brings you by, Callie?"

"I was in the neighborhood. I'm on my way to scout a possible wedding location in the graveyard."

Callie specialized in planning themed weddings—the more out there, the better. "The graveyard? How romantic."

She shrugged. "The bride wants an Anne Rice, *Interview with the Vampire*–type feeling, but elegant."

"And yet that still doesn't tell me why you're here." Although they'd ended badly ten years ago, Callie had rebuilt her life pretty much from scratch, and *that* he had to respect. Now they were in a good, but weird, place—or at least he assumed it was weird, not having any other ex-girlfriends he would now call friends. Regardless, it wasn't the kind of friendship where she would just drop by unannounced and for no reason.

She leveled a hard look at him. "I've got a big favor to ask you."

"Now is not a good time to ask me for favors. My plate is rather full at the moment."

"I know, but you know I wouldn't ask if it weren't important."

There was a fine line between being the kind of guy who was there for his friends and being a complete sucker. Why did he have a feeling he was about to be asked to cross it? "You can ask, but I don't guarantee I'll be able to do it."

"I need you to take over *The Ex Factor* for a few weeks."

She had to be kidding. *The Ex Factor* was one of the most popular items on Callie's all-things-love-and-weddings website. For some reason he'd never really understand, a column where he and his high school ex-girlfriend offered he-said-she-said advice to the lovelorn had proven wildly popular, and that popularity had helped Callie grow her fledging business into a success. He was glad he'd been able to help. "Absolutely not."

"Please, Colin? I want to go to that bridal show in Houston, and that plus everything else means I won't have a lot of spare time. I can prewrite and load some other posts, but I'll need someone to monitor the questions sent in for *Ex Factor* and answer a few."

He tried to appeal to her logic. "If you're not writing your side, it's not really an *Ex Factor* anyway. Put it on hiatus until you get back and caught up."

"It's too popular to put on hiatus. And it's a major promo tool for me. I might actually lose business if it goes dark for weeks. I've worked too hard to risk that."

Callie knew exactly where to aim. He'd gotten over the emotional part of their breakup years ago, but he'd lost respect for Callie when she'd blown that scholarship. Her determination to build her business and the way she'd done it had really been what had helped repair their friendship. He didn't want to see her lose the ground she'd fought to gain. And damn it, she knew that. "You do realize I'm trying to launch the new game, right? We're a little busy."

"You don't have to do it all yourself. You have Eric and a staff to help. I'm a one-woman show. I'm begging you." She arched an eyebrow. "Do you hear that? I'm actually *asking* for your help."

That was an old fight, one he was really tired of. He was supposed to wait until she asked for help before—as she put it—"butting into her life." But at the same time, she acted as though asking automatically meant he had to do whatever she was wanting. "Can't you just get one of your friends—one of your *girl* friends," he corrected as Callie's eyebrow went up, "to guest blog for you?"

"If I did that, I'd have to tell them who the other half of *The Ex Factor* is so y'all could communicate. Are you okay with that?"

Not many people—five, to be exact—knew he was the Ex-Man of *The Ex Factor*. He didn't need the publicity for Rainstorm, as the Venn diagram of "People Who Read Callie's Blog" and "People Who Play Zombie Apocalypse Games" didn't have a large intersection, and it might actually work against him among the gaming community if it got out. And Callie had agreed to the secret—mainly because most people would look askance at dating advice from someone they assumed was socially awkward, *Star Trek* obsessed and living in his parents' basement because he designed games. The secrecy of his identity had been played up on the blog so long that the Ex-Man was its own local celebrity. Callie had no desire to leak that info now, but a guest blogger for her would require someone else to know.

Damn it.

It would be so much easier to turn her down by email, which was most likely why Callie had come in person to ask this favor. "Let me think about it. I've got too much going on right now."

Callie started to say something else, but he stopped her. "Seriously. Not now."

Callie's head cocked to the side. "What's wrong?"

He knew exactly what she was asking—he knew her far too well not to—but he'd rather play ignorant and not go diving into his psyche at the moment. "I just told you—glitches. And they've got to be fixed before the news spreads and affects the launch."

"I know that's what you said, but things have messed up before, and there's never been a bit of code you couldn't wrangle into submission. There's something else going on with you." She sighed. "First, you blow all of us off on Fat Tuesday without any explanation—"

He rolled his eyes. "Since when do I owe you an explanation for my whereabouts?"

Callie made a face at him, but ignored the comment otherwise. "Eric says you've been grumpy for days now. What's the problem? Can I help?"

The offer was sincere, that much he knew for certain. And while he appreciated it, he had no intention of bringing any more people into this little melodrama. "Unless you have software experience that I'm unaware of—and if so, you can start taking care of your own website—I don't think you'll be much help. So…"

Callie got that worried look on her face. "It's not your mom, is it? Is she off her meds again?"

She was one of the few people on earth who would have guts enough to ask straight out like that. And the only reason she could get away with it was that she'd been there—both physically as a witness and as emotional support for him at some of the worst times. Jesus, the last thing he needed was his mother going manic right now on top of everything else. He paid a neighbor to make sure his mother took her meds, but it had been awhile since he'd checked in…

He didn't like having a memory leak in the programming to deal with, but it beat the hell out of the kind of chaos his mother could create. "No, Mom's fine."

She opened her mouth to say something else, but he cut her off with a look. Callie closed her mouth quickly. She had a certain amount of leeway—enough to ask but not enough to push the topic, and she knew it.

A second later, her eyebrows pulled together and she cocked her head. She pushed off the couch and came to perch on the edge of his desk. "What's that? It's pretty, but I don't think it's quite your style."

He looked where she was pointing, but it was totally unnecessary. Only one thing on his desk matched that description. *The cause of my bad mood.* "A watch."

"That I can see." She picked it up to examine it and let out a low whistle. "I know this brand. Is it real? Because if it is, it's not cheap."

He knew that, too. He'd had to look up the brand online, only to be more confused by the information. Jamie had seemed so *normal,* but she'd been wearing a thousand-dollar watch—or a really great knockoff—in the French Quarter on Fat Tuesday.

She smiled as though she was onto something. "It's also a *ladies'* watch. A gift, I presume?"

Damn it. Now Callie was intrigued.

The smile faded as she looked closer. "Uh-oh. Do you know the clasp is broken?"

He tried to be casual, pretending to be looking at his screen. "Yep. That's how I ended up with it."

"So you just found it on the street?" He shrugged. Callie leaned across the desk and poked him until he turned his attention to back to her. Then she just stared at him, eyes narrowed, and waited. He knew that look, and damn it, *that* was the problem with remaining friends with your ex-girlfriend. She knew too much, knew him too well, for him to get away with prevarications or vagueness. When he didn't say anything, she poked him again. "Spill."

Lie and drag this out or just tell the truth and get it over with? *Decisions.* Figuring the quickest way to get Callie off his desk would be to just tell her, he decided to tell. But not all of it. "It belongs to Jamie," he said casually.

"Jamie." She nodded. "And Jamie is…?"

"A woman I met last Tuesday in the Quarter. I missed that party because I was with her. I ended up with her watch accidentally when the clasp broke."

Callie, in love with love as always, grinned. "All day Tuesday? And you'd just met?" At his nod, she made a breathy *aw* noise before hooking a chair with her foot and pulling it close to the desk. The she leaned forward on her elbows, all excited. "Okay, I want to hear *all* about her."

Damn it. That was supposed to satisfy her, not encourage her. "Not much to tell."

"You spent all day with her, blowing off your friends in the process. There's *tons* to tell. I assume she's pretty."

"Of course."

"And…" Callie waited for him to answer, then heaved

out a sigh. "Guess we'll do this the hard way. *So*...what does she do?" she asked in a singsong voice.

"I don't know."

Callie blinked in surprise. Recovering from that, she tried again. "Where's she from?"

"I'm not sure. One of the Carolinas."

"So she was just in town for Mardi Gras?"

"Maybe. I think she said she was staying with friends, but I'm not sure. And before you ask me where, I don't know that either. Or even how long she was in town."

He could tell Callie was getting frustrated with his answers. "And her last name is..."

"Don't know."

"What the hell?" Callie sat back and crossed her arms over her chest. "Are you just *trying* to be difficult?"

"Really not." His computer chimed, and he turned his attention back to it. "Now, if you'll—"

"What *do* you know about her?"

He gave up his last bit of hope she'd just let it go and swiveled to face her. Any other time, this would be funny—baiting Callie was always fun—except he was busy and far more frustrated over this than Callie could possibly imagine.

"Let's see. She's about twenty-six, twenty-seven. Brunette, gorgeous, great legs." Callie rolled her eyes at that. "Smart, funny...a little conservative, maybe? Bourbon Street was a bit shocking for her."

"Specifics, Colin."

He thought. They'd talked about everything—and yet nothing, he realized. Instead, he rattled off what he did know. "She doesn't drink anything fruity or fancy. Her elbows are double-jointed. She knows all the words to both 'Stairway to Heaven' and 'Ice Ice Baby.' And she knows a lot about baseball."

Callie's eyebrows had gone higher with each inane detail, and when he finished, her mouth twisted. "*That's* what you know about this girl?" she asked, sarcasm dripping off each word. "She likes Led Zeppelin and baseball."

"No," he corrected. "She *knows* a lot about baseball, but I don't think she's actually a fan."

"Why?"

"Not a clue."

If he kept this up much longer, he might actually get to see Callie's head explode. "Colin Raine, I can't believe you. You spent all day with this woman and you don't even know the most basic information about her?"

Tell me something I don't already know and am not already kicking myself over. "It was Mardi Gras. We were watching parades, barhopping, dancing…you know, having *fun*." The embers deep in his belly flared up a little as he remembered exactly how much fun. "It wasn't exactly conducive to swapping life stories."

"Name, location, profession—the basic requirements of a freaking online dating profile is hardly someone's life story." She sighed and shook her head. "I'm almost afraid to ask now, but how did you end up with her watch? And don't you dare say you don't know."

That part of the story was easy enough to tell and believe. "We got caught on Bourbon at midnight. The crowds were really bad, and Jamie's really small. I was trying to get us off the street, but someone pushed between us and Jamie got pulled away from me. I had her wrist, but when the clasp on her watch broke, she slid out of it and I lost my grip. The crowd moved her away, and I couldn't find her after that."

Callie paled. She knew the dangers, the bad situations Jamie could have gotten into. "Oh, God. I hope she's okay."

"Teddy said she left a message on the Lucky Gator's answering machine—that's where I'd met her that morning when I was relieving Teddy. She says she made it home—wherever that is—safely."

"And you haven't seen or heard from her since?"

"Nope."

"Have you looked for her?"

He didn't try to hide his exasperation. "Like I can find one woman in all of New Orleans when I don't even know her last name?"

"Please tell me you at least tried."

"I waited at the Gator for over two hours that night. I figured she'd show up there. She never did." He really hated how pathetic that sounded, and it made him angry all over again.

"You said she left a message, though..."

"No last name, no number."

He could practically see the wheels turning in Callie's mind. "What about caller ID on Teddy's phone? You could match up the number to the time of the message..."

He was shaking his head even as she spoke. "Teddy's phone only holds the last ten numbers. It was gone by the time I checked."

"Then call the phone company—"

"Let it go, Callie." He'd played amateur detective for two days, even tracking down the band and the guitar player David, hoping for a lead to Kelsey. David hadn't even remembered Kelsey's name, so that was a bust. And although she'd left that message, he'd still called a friend at NOPD and had him check the jails, the hospitals, even the morgue. No one matching Jamie's description. He was out of ideas. And it turned out the phone company didn't like to give out that kind of information without a warrant. "She knows my name, and she knew to call the Gator to get a message to me. If she wants to find me, she can." The fact she hadn't really ticked him off. She hadn't gone back to the bar in the following days. And it didn't seem as if she was trying to find him. Hell, if she'd even bothered to look him up on Google, he'd have popped up as the very first result. He'd checked.

"I can't just let it go, Colin."

"I have, so you might as well. She's probably gone back to wherever by now."

"You don't know that. She said she made it home safe, so that probably means she was staying with friends who live here, not in a hotel." Callie stood and began pacing. "If she was with friends, there's a good chance it was a long vacation and she's still in town. If not, maybe we could find the friends she was staying with." She put her hand on her chest dramatically. "We can find your Cinderella. We have to."

"My what?"

"A chance meeting, separated at midnight, and all you have is something she left behind accidentally... It's the Cinderella story."

He was wrong. He should have stuck with a lie. Or silence. Silence would have been good. "Callie, honey, step back from the fairy tales."

She made a face at him. "Granted, you're not exactly Prince Charming, but..."

He lost his last shred of patience. "Just drop it, Callie," he snapped. Her hurt and shocked look had him feeling bad for that almost immediately. "I appreciate your concern, but there's nothing to be done, so it doesn't make any sense to keep worrying over it."

"You can't Dr. Spock your way out of this."

"What?"

"Logic and reason don't apply here. You're a man, not a Vulcan."

"You're thinking of Mr. Spock," he corrected. "Dr. Spock is the baby guy."

She waved a hand. "Whatever. You liked this girl enough at the time, but not enough to try to find her now?"

"It seems rather fruitless, and I don't have time for fruitless."

"What? So you're just going to keep that watch?" she challenged. "Finders, keepers, or some such?"

He shrugged. "If she wants it back, she'll contact me."

"What if she can't? What if…what if…what if she got mugged on the way home, hit her head and has amnesia now?"

Oh, dear God. "Okay, I'm going back to the *Dungeons of Zhorg,* where memory issues are a *real* thing." To soften the blow, he added, "Thanks, though."

Callie's mouth twisted, but she let the subject drop. "Want to go to lunch?"

As if he was going to subject himself to another hour of Callie's questions about Jamie. He pointed to his computer. "Trolls. Dragons. They need me."

"Okay." Finally getting the message, she grabbed her bag and put it over her shoulder. "Sorry about your mystery lady."

He shrugged. "It happens. Ships passing in the night and all that." *Keep telling yourself that.*

"It *is* a great story, though. Like the beginning of a book or something."

Callie was a romantic who spent way too much time indulging people's fantasies. She'd stew on this if he didn't nip it in the bud now. "Just an interesting foot-note for my biography."

Callie was finally headed for the door. "Good luck fixing the trolls," she called over her shoulder.

He was going to need it. Although Colin tried to focus on the code, thoughts of Jamie kept forcing their way back in, distracting him. Most of it was simple, ridiculous, moony teenager stuff—the way her nose crinkled when she laughed, her triumphant joy at catching a doubloon in one hand, the way she'd gamely tried to eat a muffuletta bigger than her own head—but those innocent images quickly gave way to much more adult images, and *those* were much harder to get out of his head because they came with full sensory memories that affected him physically as well as mentally.

He could still taste her, feel her...

Argh. He shifted in his chair. He needed his blood flowing to his brain right now, not his lap. "Memory leak. Lost revenue. Angry gamers." Jamie had been an aberration, an interlude, a time out from the norm.

One perfect, amazing day with an amazing woman. He should just be happy it had happened. It would give him something fun to think back on when he was old and in the nursing home.

He fingered the watch, and Callie's over-romantic ideas came rushing back.

Maybe...

He didn't get to finish the thought, because a message from Eric popped up on his screen at that moment with the two most beautiful words inside: FOUND IT.

Aside from the jubilation, it was another, more forceful reminder that this daydreaming was a waste of time. He dropped Jamie's watch into his desk drawer and closed it.

If he could get Callie, of all people, to drop it and move on, he could do it, too.

It was that simple.

But he should have known it wouldn't be that simple. Because three days later, Callie's extra-special edition of *The Ex Factor* went viral.

CHAPTER FOUR

Jamie cursed under her breath as the brush slipped and left a streak of Moody Mauve across the top of her thumb. Ah, how quickly she'd gotten used to paying other people for things like manicures.

Her bank account wasn't in dire straits just yet, but until things got settled, she couldn't waste money on things she could do herself. She allowed herself one brief wistful memory of the Ivy Spa and their amazing staff, who included a mimosa and a scalp massage with every mani-pedi.

She'd gotten spoiled so quickly. After seasons of barely getting by as Joey was making next to nothing in the minor league, the jump to the major league had felt like a lottery win. Then Joey had signed a couple of endorsement deals, and she'd discovered the stores on Rodeo Drive and Fifth Avenue. Joey had called her his princess and encouraged her to live the part.

So she had.

And while she truly believed she was doing the right thing now and was proud of herself for doing it, she wasn't ashamed to say she missed it.

But she had two job interviews lined up—one to-morrow and one the day after—and if all went well, maybe one day she'd be able to afford some of those little luxuries again—even if Prada would never be in her budget again.

Sometimes she wondered if her pride and self-respect had been worth what she had traded for them.

And she'd traded back and forth a lot.

But this was the right thing, she reminded herself. Money was like a drug and she was just detoxing. It wasn't as though she was in danger of starving or living in a box under the bridge. Ninety-nine percent of the world lived without valet service and scalp massages. She could, too.

She was thinking positive thoughts about her interview tomorrow, even though her résumé was a bit thin. "Arm Candy" wasn't exactly a skill set that excited potential employers, and the gaps in her employment history were going to be hard to explain, too. At least she had *some* experience—she *had* worked for a while—but between that and the rather questionable ethics situation she'd been embroiled in—however accidentally or unwillingly—it might be tough to find a business willing to trust her too much.

The crows of doom were perched on her shoulders again, and she gave herself a strong mental shake as she went back to her manicure. *I can do this. Put positive energy out to the universe and positive things will return to me.*

Kelsey's apartment in the Warehouse District was tiny, but well kept and seemingly safe. And since Jamie didn't own much stuff, the tininess didn't matter. While she and Kelsey didn't have much in common, they were getting along well enough. Granted, it helped that Kelsey worked odd hours as a nurse, but when she *was* home, she spent a lot of time on the computer and didn't really care what

Jamie watched on TV. *Housing — check.* Job was next on the list, and after that, the world would be her oyster.

That was the plan, at least.

She blew on her nails, pleased with her efforts. *Not too shabby,* she thought, and placed another little check mark in her mental list of accomplishments. Joey had used to say—and not completely teasingly either—that her idea of roughing it was doing her own nails, yet here she was. "Proving Joey Wrong" was a large category, but she was chipping away at it bit by bit.

Kelsey was in the recliner, eyes on her laptop and ears covered by a set of large black headphones, so Jamie let the *Law & Order* marathon drone on without much guilt. She was debating another coat of polish when Kelsey took her headphones off.

"Hey, Jamie, do you know anything about the Zephyrs?"

The question came so far out of left field that Jamie nearly dropped the polish bottle she was holding between her knees. She didn't really know much about Kelsey, but she hadn't mentioned baseball at all until this moment. And since Kelsey didn't know about her past—just that she'd come out of a long-term relationship, but not with whom or why—it was an odd question, indeed. "Um, they're the triple-A affiliate for the Marlins, they've got some good players... Why?"

"If I got tickets, would you want to go?"

"God, no." She'd been the perfect athlete girlfriend, always in her spot at every game, cheering as loudly as she could, but the honest truth was that she abhorred everything about baseball. She'd rather watch paint dry. Breaking up with Joey had meant she'd never have to spend another minute of her life at the ball field, and *that* knowledge had helped buoy her through the worst of it.

Belatedly realizing how her refusal might be considered rude—assuming Kelsey was trying to broach new avenues of friendship or shared interests—she tried to soften it. "I mean, thanks, but I'm not really a fan."

Kelsey nodded. A second later, she asked, "Are you double-jointed?"

What the hell? Did Kelsey have some kind of weird disorder? *Wonder if the hospital knows.* "Yeah, my elbows. Why?"

Over the top of the computer screen, Kelsey smiled. "Just wondering. By the way, do you know what time it is?"

Time for me to be looking for a different place to live? The girl had a computer on her lap and a cell phone balanced on the arm of her chair, and she was asking Jamie what time it was? "Sorry, no. Maybe a little after ten?"

"No watch, huh?"

"I lost mine."

"I see. How interesting."

If Kelsey was crazy, better to find out now. "How is that interesting?"

Kelsey closed the laptop. "I know you're new in town, but have you heard of *The Ex Factor*?"

"The TV show? Of course."

Kelsey shook her head. "No. *Ex* as in ex-boyfriend."

"Then no, I haven't."

"It's an online column run by a local girl who does wedding planning. She and her ex-boyfriend do a little thing a few times a month where they give different perspectives on an issue or a question that's sent in. It's hugely popular, and the kind of thing that everyone will be talking about at work the next day."

And? "It sounds cute. I'll check it out one day."

Kelsey passed the laptop her way. "Actually, you might want to check it out now."

Carefully, so as not to mess up her nails, Jamie took the computer and flipped it open. She wasn't sure what she was supposed to be looking at, but it seemed like a basic website, with a cartoon drawing of a man and a woman back to back and a *The Ex Factor* banner between them.

The headline, in a very large font, read, A Real Cinderella Story, and the paragraph beneath started, "Once upon a time, in the French Quarter on Fat Tuesday…"

No.

Something akin to dread settled into her chest.

By the end of the first paragraph, the pieces fell into place. Adrenaline surged through her veins. "Oh, my sweet God."

The horror only got worse as she scanned the article. While thankfully rather skinny on the details, there was the story of what, until this moment, had seemed like the best day of her life. Something she could think back on fondly and relish the memory.

It had been a private, happy story, one she hadn't shared with anyone simply because she'd wanted to keep it to herself. But it seemed to be news somehow, and based on the counter at the bottom of the page, it was now *everyone's* business.

It was all there: how they were separated at midnight, leaving her Prince Charming with her watch instead of a glass slipper. A physical description of her and those details Kelsey had been checking—like the fact she had extensive baseball knowledge but didn't enjoy the game and her double-jointed elbows. It ended with a plea for anyone who knew "Cinderella Jamie" to please contact someone named Callie with the info.

That gave her pause. A second, less panicked look at the article showed her that it didn't mention Colin by name or description, simply calling him Prince Charming and providing little detail to his identity.

Kelsey snorted again. "That is you. Don't deny it."

Jamie wondered if she possibly could. She looked over to see Kelsey messing with her phone.

"I remember you taking his picture and putting his name into my phone in case he turned out to be an ax murderer or something," Kelsey muttered, "but now I can't find it."

And you never will. Wednesday morning, after deciding it would be best if she didn't contact Colin again, she'd deleted both his picture and his name from Kelsey's phone while Kelsey was in the shower. She'd felt a little silly doing it, but now she was thankful for her forethought.

"Damn it, why can't I find it?"

Jamie let that question pass. She was on the internet. *Again.* No one in town knew her and there was no reason anyone—even those who followed sports obsessively—would recognize her from the description here, but still.... She didn't want to be notorious again. Ever.

But Kelsey had figured it out. Eventually she would make friends here, and what if one of them managed to put it together? Although it wasn't specifically stated in the article, the subtext was that she'd hooked up with Prince Charming, and now she looked like a slut. Or maybe that was just her own guilty conscience talking. "You say this *Ex Factor* thing is pretty popular?"

Kelsey's amused look turned to pity. "*Very* popular. And this article has gone viral. I doubt there's anyone in New Orleans under the age of sixty who hasn't heard about it."

And now she had to go job hunting in this atmosphere. Sweet Jesus, maybe she should just move. At least she wasn't even fully unpacked yet. Of course, there was the slim hope that this would all die down quickly—the internet was fickle and had a short attention span.

Dignity and distance. If she'd learned anything from that three-ring circus Joey had dragged her into, she knew how best to handle this. Do not acknowledge. Do not deny. Everything she said would be held against her, so it was best to say nothing. She forced herself to shrug casually and handed the laptop back to Kelsey.

"That's it?" Kelsey asked. "Aren't you excited that Prince Charming is looking for you?"

"Not like this, no." She wanted privacy, not notoriety.

"At least tell me who he is."

She tried to sound casual. "Nobody."

"Bull. You ditched me to spend the day with him. You liked him. And I do remember he was pretty damn cute, too."

Kelsey had ditched her—mentally at least—long before Colin had come into the picture, but she let that slide. "Look, I really don't need to go rushing into anything with anyone right now. I'm still finding my feet here." But Kelsey's fingers were already flying across the keyboard. There was a flutter of panic in her chest. "You're not emailing that Callie person, are you?"

Kelsey paused and grinned over the screen. "Want me to?"

"No."

"Pity. I'm just checking out what other people are saying."

"I don't want to know." Jamie pushed against the laptop gently, bringing the screen down, but not all the way onto Kelsey's fingers. "I'm asking you to please just let this go. Don't tell anyone you know who Cinderella is and let it die down. Believe me when I say that I have my reasons, and simply let it go at that."

"But he's looking for you."

"So? Maybe I don't want to be found."

"Did he turn out to be a jerk? Get creepy?"

Try as she might, she couldn't lie about it. "No, nothing like that. I just don't really need for it to be any more than it was."

Kelsey huffed. "Well, don't you at least want your watch back? I remember it's pretty. Looked expensive, too."

The watch had been a gift from Joey, a grand gesture when he'd signed with his first minor-league team and a promise of much nicer things to come, but it didn't hold any sentimental value to her now. In fact, it seemed more symbolic to just let it go, like a shackle that she'd freed herself from as she started over. "No. I never really liked it anyway."

"Well, hell, you could have given it to me," Kelsey grumbled.

Kelsey had oohed and ahhed over her clothes and her shoes as she'd unpacked, assuming they were fakes and wanting to know where Jamie shopped to find the "good stuff." Jamie hadn't corrected her, not wanting to admit that while she was cash poor, she was wardrobe rich. Tomorrow she'd be wearing a Gucci skirt and her lucky Louboutins while looking for a job that she hoped would pay enough to cover her rent. *Oh, the irony.*

Jamie pushed to her feet and packed up her manicure supplies. "I'm going to bed. I have interviews tomorrow."

"You're crazy, you know. You land in town like a refugee and immediately meet a hottie who's now pining for you. I've lived here my whole life and nada. It's not fair."

For the sake of homestead harmony, she had to answer that. "Surely there are some cute doctors at the hospital," she offered optimistically.

"You'd think, but sadly, no."

She and Kelsey weren't really friends, so Jamie wasn't sure whether to provide sympathy or encouragement. And with her background, she certainly wasn't qualified to offer dating advice of any sort. She went with the lame but true, "Pity."

"That it is."

"Good night, Kels."

While she'd claimed disinterest to Kelsey, now that she was alone in her tiny bedroom, she started to have second thoughts. She'd liked Colin—liked him a lot, actually—and had they not parted so abruptly, she probably would have ended up giving him a phone number and planned to see him again. But in the last week, she'd gotten accustomed to the idea that it was a one-off, and something about it had given her some much-needed confidence.

And she really didn't like the fact that their day was now plastered across the internet. It cheapened the whole thing, somehow.

Last week she'd seen the way they'd parted as a sign from the universe they just weren't meant to be. She could assume the article was another sign, but it was hard to tell what kind of sign it was. A nudge to get her to contact Colin? Or a very public reminder guaranteed to make her want to stay away?

She had made so many decisions recently and she was tired of second-and third-guessing herself all the time trying to figure out what to do.

Fighting the temptation to pull out her laptop and look Colin up online was tough, but she managed to win that battle for the moment. It seemed best to stick with her original plan and let Colin remain a happy memory. Should she change her mind, he'd be easy enough to find.

Her interview outfit was hanging on the back of her bedroom door. It caused her stomach to knot up, reminding her that she had too much riding on decisions to risk making the wrong one. And she certainly couldn't afford to let her hormones weigh in on those decisions.

She had enough on her plate right now. No sense adding more.

He had to give Callie credit: the girl knew how to light a fire. Unfortunately, the flames were getting out of hand.

It seemed everyone really did love a Cinderella story.

And he'd never been so glad that he'd never put his name on *The Ex Factor*. Speculations—on Callie's blog, the other sites that'd reblogged the story and the sites just commenting on the situation—were that the Ex-Man was Prince Charming.

And since the Ex-Man had his own email address listed right there on *The Ex Factor* page, it hadn't taken too long for his in-box to explode.

That was how he'd found out about Callie's article. He'd been tempted to pull down the article—if not the entire site—in retaliation, but that would only feed that speculation that Prince Charming and Ex-Man were one and the same. And it wouldn't really accomplish much anyway now; the story was already out there, taking on a life of its own.

No one had come forward with any information about Jamie, but it seemed there were plenty of women ready and willing to take her place in this freaky fairy tale. He had hundreds of messages, pictures, offers—some very scary, possibly-illegal-in-some-states offers—and his in-box probably contained more naked breasts than Bourbon Street on Fat Tuesday.

If he wanted a date, he had his choice of women.

It was more than a little mind-blowing. Callie had always insisted that he didn't *look* like a typical geek, and he'd long fought against the stereotype, but stereotypes wouldn't be stereotypes unless they had some truth to them. Women were often interested in him—until he told them what he did, and then they seemed to be put off by the worry he might be into freaky cosplay or quote Yoda to them.

Added to that was the sheer number of hours he'd spent developing *No Quarter* while still holding down a job to pay his rent.... Well, there hadn't been a lot of time available for dating anyway.

So while he hadn't lived the life of a monk, he wasn't exactly master of the dating universe, either. And while he was semi-famous in the gaming community, he wasn't exactly a celebrity, so the attentions of a horde of women were a little disconcerting.

Even more so was the fact none of these women knew for certain who he was.

And even if he *did* want the attention, now was not a great time. They were less than three weeks away from the release date, and his attention really needed to be on *Dungeons of Zhorg*.

Eric was really the face and voice of Rainstorm—he looked the part, a perfect hipster geek who could enthuse with the very best of them, and the true geeks could relate to him better—so the PR was mostly on him. That kept him busy enough that Colin hadn't seen him in days while he played the code monkey, troubleshooting and patching. It was a good distribution of labor—and one that he quite liked—but being trapped at his computer made the distraction of his in-box almost too much—like a train wreck he couldn't *not* watch.

If Callie had stopped to think for even a second before plastering his private life across the internet—however pseudoanonymously—she'd have realized her little article had the potential to turn into a freakin' circus. And she, probably more than anyone, knew how much he hated the chaos. She'd been there in some of the worst times, when his mom was so depressed she couldn't get out of bed or so manic she was bouncing off the walls, and he'd been left wandering through the rubble. *She'd* been the one to pull him out of his games and back into the real world, giving moral support as he tried to get it all under control.

So the fact she'd intentionally created chaos in his personal life—*especially* at a time when he had plenty on his plate already.... Well, obviously she hadn't thought it through—or else she simply didn't care anymore and would do anything to bring publicity to her blog.

They were supposedly friends these days, but with friends like that...*Jesus*.

Around noon, he heard a quiet knock on his door. Figuring it was Elise, whom he'd promised to take to lunch, he didn't bother turning around. "Give me five minutes."

"Five minutes is really all I need."

The voice slammed into him and his fingers froze. Composing himself, he turned slowly in his chair.

Jamie.

Only it wasn't quite the Jamie he remembered. Mardi Gras Jamie had been a wholesome girl-next-door kind of sexy, but the expensive-looking woman at his door was far from the girl next door. That rich chestnut hair curled around an expertly made-up face in soft waves. A silky blouse tucked into a high-waisted black skirt that skimmed straight down the legs he remembered so well and stopped just short of her knee. The black stiletto pumps that straddled the line between sexy and serviceable did funny things to his stomach. It was Jamie, no doubt there, but the polished and poised woman in front of him had him rethinking what little he thought he knew about her.

But he did know this woman intimately, something his little brain was reminding him of rather earnestly, but her composed face and stiff attitude were an icy wet blanket on that.

"Hi, Colin."

The simple greeting snapped him back to the present and he wondered how long he'd been staring at her. "This is a surprise."

Jamie's eyebrow quirked up and he realized that had come out sharper than intended. "The young woman out front told me to just come in." Her mouth twisted. "She did ask to see my elbows first, though. Jeez, does everyone know you're Prince Charming?"

"Elise is my sister. Of course she knows. Otherwise, not many people do." He leaned back in his chair. Jamie's face was unreadable—she didn't look happy to see him, but she didn't look *un*happy, either. And since he hadn't planned for Callie's stunt to actually work, he hadn't prepared himself for the possibility that it might. Then again, he hadn't expected her to show up unannounced if it *did,* either. Seems she'd looked him up after all. "I was beginning to think something bad had happened to you the other night."

A tiny crease formed between her eyebrows. "Did you not get my message? I left one at the Lucky Gator."

That familiar mixture of anger and frustration came back. She'd *wanted* to disappear. Hell, the fact she was here now was proof she hadn't left town or anything, so her lack of even a half-assed attempt to find him until now was insulting. "Oh, I got it. It was the lack of any other contact that caused concern."

"Well, I'm sorry for that—worrying you, that is." She shifted a small black bag to the opposite arm and looked around. "You're not a bartender at the Lucky Gator."

"No." Was that why she hadn't gotten in touch before now? She thought he was just a bartender? "Does that matter?"

"No, of course not. It was just a bit of a surprise." After another pointed look around, she asked, "If this is your business, why were you bartending?"

That was her burning question? "Teddy's a friend. He needed some help that day."

"But you let me think you worked there."

"You didn't actually ask, so I didn't offer. And rethinking that experience has made me realize that you weren't exactly forthcoming with personal details, either."

"True," she agreed, but she didn't offer an explanation as to why. "I want you to know, Colin, that I had a really great time with you that day."

"I can tell."

"Don't be like that."

"Like what, Jamie? One minute you're all over me and the next you drop off the face of the earth."

She straightened her shoulders. "And I'm sorry about that. I didn't handle the situation well, but…" She sighed. "It's just not a good time for me to get seriously involved with anyone."

"Whoa, there. That's jumping a bit ahead, don't you think?"

She shook her head. "It's not personal. You seem like a great guy."

He didn't want nor need to listen to the it's-not-you-it's-me spiel. He was neither a masochist nor that fragile. He certainly didn't need a date that badly. Hell, he had a whole in-box of women who wanted him sight unseen—and didn't seem to care what he did for a living.

After a week of wondering and worrying, this was not at all what he'd pictured their reunion would be but Jamie's attitude was cold and distant, as if she was a one-night stand he'd neglected to call the next day.

Which was quite ironic, now that he thought about it.

But what had he expected, really?

Screw it. "I'll get your watch."

"What?"

He opened the drawer where he'd stuck her watch the other day and pulled it out. As he walked around the desk, he held it out to her. "Your watch. I assume that's what you came for."

The watch suited *this* Jamie—expensive, well-coiffed, aloof—further adding to the mystery. She reached for it and their hands touched for a second. It sent a shiver of electricity and excitement up his arm, giving his temporarily tamped-down libido a jolt of awakening. Jamie, though, practically recoiled from the contact, pulling away quickly as though she'd been burned.

Enough was enough. "Unless there's something else, I really need to get back to work."

"Actually, that's not why I came."

"If you're not here to get seriously involved—" he nearly choked on the words "—and you're not here for your watch, why are you here?"

Her eyes flashed, calling him an ass without saying a word. Then she took a deep breath and seemed to compose herself. "I'll make this quick, since I know you're busy. I need you to make this Cinderella crap stop."

Ah, so that's what pulled her out of hiding. "I'm not sure I can. And even if I could, why do you even care?"

Clearly exasperated, she stalked over to his couch and sat. "I had a job interview this morning, Colin. When the HR person saw that I was brunette and named Jamie, she laughed and asked me if I was your Cinderella. I was too horrified to deny it quick enough, and she was rather shocked to realize I was. Needless to say, since your little article didn't paint me in the most flattering light, it was a very uncomfortable interview, and I doubt I'll be getting a second one."

The fact she was job hunting meant not only had she not left town, she wasn't planning to, either. The frustration and anger spiked again. What else had she been less than truthful about? "Not my article," he corrected. "That was all Callie. I didn't know about it until after."

"I'll admit I'm glad it wasn't you who wrote it. But that doesn't change the fact that it's out there. Announce you've found her or that you made it up as a joke, something, *anything* to make people quit talking about it."

Granted, this was an annoying mess, but Jamie seemed way too upset over it. Especially considering that there was no way to prove—aside from her elbows—that she was the Jamie in question. "You're overreacting just a little, don't you think?"

"I just got out of a relationship that ended in the most ugly way imaginable." While he'd normally dismiss a statement like that as hyperbole, there was an undertone to her words that made him believe it. "I moved here to get away from all that and start fresh. Now I've got a reputation to live down and I've barely had time to unpack yet."

He had his pride and Jamie was doing a damn good job trying to dent it. As juvenile as it was, it made him less willing to swing into action—even if he *could* push back against it, which was questionable. "It will fade away on its own. That's the nature of these things."

"I know that. But it doesn't really help me now. When I'm job hunting."

He could mention that this wasn't really an ideal time for him either, but other than the inconvenience of it, he really couldn't say it was a bad thing. For him. He lost nothing letting it play out.

At the same time, he knew how hard it was to build something, to make something of yourself. He'd been in a similar place before, feeling as if the world was spinning out of control, with no one to lean on for support, his future in jeopardy and too many people looking to him to sort out their problems.

He sincerely doubted Jamie's situation was anywhere near as dire, but she seemed to believe it was, and he couldn't be a party to sabotaging anyone's attempts to straighten their life out and rebuild. He leaned back against his desk and sighed. "Fine. You just keep denying it's you to anyone who asks—and don't show them your elbows—and I'll get the word out that the mystery lady has been found. In Utah or something. I have some blogger friends who might be able to help spread that news."

Jamie seemed to slump a little in relief. "Thank you. I appreciate that." After a moment of silence, she cleared her throat. "Look, Colin—"

This whole conversation bordered on insane, and it wasn't helping his blood pressure any, either. "Unless there's something else," he interrupted, "I'm going to get back to work."

"Right. Thanks. Bye, Colin." With a half smile that looked strained at best, she left.

Well, so much for Callie's fairy-tale dreams. After all

that buildup, this result was both anticlimactic and frustrating. What was crazy was that he almost felt disappointed it had turned out like this.

Hell, he was just lucky it wasn't worse somehow.

Jamie wanted to kick herself. She'd acted like a cold bitch—a persona she'd perfected over the last few months—but she felt terrible about it. Both because she could tell she'd hurt Colin's feelings the other night—which only partly excused his piss-poor attitude—and because she got the weird feeling she was walking away from something she shouldn't.

Something important. Which made no sense at all.

She hadn't been prepared for the very visceral reaction she'd had to seeing him again. She'd played him down in her head as much as she could, convincing herself she'd just been caught up in the party atmosphere and fueled by cheap beer.

And it had been working—until about fifteen minutes ago, when he'd turned around looking even yummier than she remembered and causing her to wobble dangerously on her shoes. She'd been *this close* to crawling across his desk.

Thank God she hadn't, because none of that charm she remembered had been on display today. In fact, Colin had a bit of a dickish streak she hadn't seen before.

So everything seemed to be stacking up to tell her this wasn't a good idea. Even if she wanted to ignore the messages the universe had sent by separating them that evening, now they were notorious.

She just wanted to be a private citizen again, because notoriety sucked. She'd had a taste of it as Joey's fiancée—once he'd gone pro in such a big way, she'd been on his arm at some pretty major, and heavily photographed, events. That had led to a small interest by a few paparazzi and blogs, but only on slow news days. But then the scandal had broken. The investigation, the allegations, the whole dirty mess had played out far too publicly, and she'd been dragged straight into the middle of the mess.

Then the same press that'd posted what she was wearing and where she was lunching had turned on her. First mocking her for naïveté when she defended Joey, then vilifying her when she turned against him.

She wasn't willingly going to insert herself into any kind of media anything. She just needed to work on her acting skills and learn how to laugh off the Cinderella question—if it came up again—and hopefully the news that Ex-Man's Cinderella was happily up in Utah now might slow some of that down.

Ugh. Who'd want to be Cinderella anyway? She hated all those stupid fairy tales—simpering little princesses who just waited around for a prince to come solve all their problems for them.

It was insulting, really.

She'd spent too much of her life acting like one of those princesses, letting things happen to her and around her and never taking control.

Look where that had landed her.

She'd had quite enough of Cinderella, thanks very much. She didn't need Colin to take care of this.

She'd come to New Orleans to take control of her own life, and by God, that was exactly what she was going to do.

Starting right now.

CHAPTER FIVE

See, I don't want that fairy tale. I don't want a
Prince Charming to make all my dreams come
true. *I* want to make my dreams come true. No
one should try to make their happily ever after de-
pendent upon the actions of someone else. Nothing
against Prince Charming, of course.

ERIC ACTUALLY LAUGHED out loud at the last line. "Someone certainly stirred her up with a big ol' stick."

The extra-special "Cinderella Speaks" edition of *The
Ex Factor* was garnering almost as much attention as the
original article. Only this time, Jamie's rant against pas-
sive princesses had been picked up by every girl power
blogger on the internet and hailed as the newest femi-
nist manifesto.

Callie could have at least *warned* him first. "This has
gotten way out of hand," he grumbled.

"You're not taking this personally, are you?"

Colin pulled a beer out of the cooler and went back to
check the grill. The small staff of Rainstorm Games, the
various other contractors who'd worked on *Zhorg* and a
few friends were milling around in small groups across
Eric's yard and porch as they celebrated the upcoming

launch. "Being made to look like a jackass for the amusement of the entire city? Yeah, a little."

"First off, except for a few friends, no one even knows it's you. So calm down."

"*I* know. And that's enough."

"And you care why, exactly?"

Colin didn't have a good answer for that question.

Eric shrugged as he slipped his phone back into his pocket. "Let Callie and Jamie have their little moment. What difference does it really make?"

Eric was right. Jamie obviously had issues—deep, personal, crazy issues—none of which really had anything to do with him. The last thing he needed in his life was another loose cannon to run damage control around.

"By the way," Eric added, "I should probably tell you she's here."

"Who?"

"Jamie."

"What?"

Eric shrugged apologetically. "Elise invited Callie, and Callie asked if she could bring a friend. Turns out that friend is Jamie. They got here about twenty minutes ago."

Sweet Jesus. When had Callie and Jamie bonded? He looked around, easily spotting Callie's blond hair. Jamie was next to her, all smiles as Callie introduced her to people. In another chameleon-like change, this Jamie was neither the girl next door of Fat Tuesday nor the chic sophisticate who'd stared him down in his office last week. Instead, she looked earthy and natural with her hair piled loosely atop her head, exposing the line of her neck and shoulders. A colorful sundress emphasized her breasts before flowing to her calves.

It seemed this look did it for him, too, as the heat from the grill had nothing on the heat rising off him.

What was it about her? Sure, physically she checked all his boxes, but he wasn't some horny teenager who couldn't control himself around a pretty woman. And if he'd developed some kind of new yen for unavailable crazy women, he needed to know now so he could find a good therapist.

Whatever it was, he needed to get it under control, because Callie was headed toward him with Jamie in tow, ready to wreak more havoc on his life.

She introduced Jamie first to Eric, who managed to keep a straight face. *Just.*

"Congratulations on your launch, and thank you for letting me crash your party." Jamie's smile was both genuine and charming and it worked on Eric perfectly.

"No, thank *you* for coming," Eric gushed, making Colin want to hit him hard. "We don't get nearly enough pretty women around here. I warn you, though, this crowd could turn very geeky at any moment. You might regret coming."

Jamie smiled. "That's a risk I'm willing to take."

Callie laughed. "This crowd can't *turn* geeky. It's geek central already. And you already know our head geek, Colin."

Jamie's smile dimmed a little, becoming slightly self-conscious. "Hi."

Callie looped her arm through Eric's. "Why don't you show me where the beer is?"

It was a transparent ploy, as Callie had been to dozens of parties at Eric's and knew damn well exactly where the coolers were. Eric, though, grabbed the excuse and led her away before Colin had a chance to call them on it.

So that left him alone with Jamie. "I can't say I expected to see you here."

"I know. But I don't know many people yet, so I

jumped at the chance to actually get out and meet some. I'm going a little stir crazy."

"Eric wasn't kidding though. Geek central." He was very proud of himself. Even as his body was screaming at him to touch her, he was able to keep himself calm and even detached-sounding. She couldn't make him crazy if he didn't let her.

"Everyone has something they go geek for. I'm not one to judge on what that thing is." Her mouth twisted. "As long as it's not sports, that is."

"I can safely say that sports aren't real popular with this crowd."

"I'm very happy to hear it. And I'd like to apologize," she said in the same breath.

He had to shift focus quickly. "For what?"

"Being such a bitch the other day."

He wasn't sure how to respond to that. "Well, it got your point across."

"I know, but I'm not normally like that. My only excuse is that I don't like to feel like my life is out of my control. The chaos scares the crap out of me and it seems I don't handle that well."

Few people did. Hell, he'd been ruled by that fear for years, always trying to stay ahead of whatever disaster might be coming down the pike next as his mom swung from extreme to extreme, dragging him and Elise along for the ride.

Jamie squared her shoulders. "So I'm not going to wait around anymore for someone else to come fix my problems."

He could relate. He'd learned to cope—eventually—mainly by getting past that fear and taking control of what he could. Jamie had gotten there a little quicker than most. "You made that clear in your rebuttal on the blog."

"No one seemed to be interested in the whole she's-in-Utah thing, so I decided to be proactive. So I wrote it up and emailed Callie through the site. Hopefully that will put an end to the Cinderella thing and you, me and *The Ex Factor* can go back to business as usual."

"You told him already?" Callie reappeared with beers and handed one to Jamie. "Excellent."

Her cheerfulness put him on guard. "Told me what?"

"That you're off the hook. I took your advice and I found a guest blogger." The smile grew bigger, and slightly mocking, as well. "Jamie's going to cover for me—since you wouldn't—and depending on how that goes, may become a regular." She lifted an eyebrow in his direction. "Jamie already knows your secret identity, so no worries there. Is that going to be a problem?"

He looked at Jamie, who seemed to have developed a great interest in the label of her beer, then back to Callie. *Damn it.* "Of course not."

"Good." She held out a plate. "Can I have a burger?"

He cursed. He'd been distracted by Jamie's arrival, and now the burgers were slightly overdone. Talk about needing to get things back under control. He had no idea why Jamie had the ability to distract him like this, but his brain seemed to check out whenever she was around.

The burned burgers were simply another indication that it would be better for his mental health—not to mention his career and cooking skills—to pretend he'd never met the woman.

She must have had similar feelings, as Jamie spent most of the evening at a distance. But he was painfully aware of her presence nonetheless, almost as if he was catching whiffs of her pheromones, and the resulting level of distraction had people assuming he'd had too much to drink and threatening to confiscate his car keys.

All because of one unavailable crazy woman.

Maybe he should start looking for that therapist.

A cookout, some beers, people hanging out and having a good time…Jamie couldn't remember the last time she'd spent such a normal evening.

Well, *normal* might not be quite the right word. She'd been warned of potential geekiness, and it hadn't been a false alarm. These were people who lived and breathed technology, and she spent a good portion of the evening in conversations that she didn't quite understand—and that sometimes didn't even sound like English—but she'd never been ridiculed for her lack of knowledge, and more than once people had patiently tried to explain things to her. They also had a fascination with sections of pop culture totally outside of her expertise or experience, but beyond being offered DVD sets of TV shows she simply "had to watch," she'd come through unscathed.

She'd spent a large part of her life around jocks and was pleasantly surprised to find that for all of the jocks-versus-geeks jokes, the situations weren't that much different—especially for those who weren't as excited or knowledgeable about the topic. Both crowds spoke in a mixture of acronyms and numbers and often got very excited about the minute details of the oddest things.

And since none of these people followed sports, she didn't have to worry about them having an opinion on Joey and his current troubles. It never even came up. A night without any discussion of baseball was such a refreshing change, she didn't care that she hadn't understood much of the rest of the conversation.

While this wasn't quite what she'd expected—or even begun to imagine—from her move to New Orleans, she wasn't unhappy, either. She'd tripped at the start line, but all in all, had managed to recover okay. And she'd made a couple of new friends as well.

Maybe she had been meant to meet Colin. Colin had led her to Callie—who was now talking about maybe paying her to blog regularly if things went well—and this group of people who'd welcomed her without missing a beat.

But Colin…*that* was a problem.

She stole a peek over to where Colin was talking with a small group. That cold, snippy Colin from the other day at his office was missing, and he was pure relaxed charm tonight. He had plenty of friends, and even Callie—his ex, for goodness' sake—seemed to like him, so that attitude obviously wasn't a large part of his personality.

He was definitely a bit of a chimera. That brawn belied some serious brains—not only when it came to computers and games and how they all worked, but also the business side. In an instant he could flip, though, arguing about the physics of *Doctor Who* in one breath and the hotness of the current companion the next. He was someone who seemed comfortable in his own skin.

She envied him that a little.

However, she did rather wish she hadn't had sex with Colin. No, that wasn't quite right. The sex had been great, and she couldn't regret that. It was more the fact that she'd had sex with him *already. That* fact made things a little awkward. Aside from the mental images that popped into her head at inopportune moments, she had some kind of residual energy from him that, even now, nearly two weeks later after the fact, *still* caused tingly shivers.

And possibly because this was such an inappropriate place and time, she couldn't *not* think about the details she'd been brutally suppressing—the way she'd just been overwhelmed by want, desperate with need, ending up with the kind of orgasm she'd heard rumors of but never experienced.

Damn it. She felt another flush coming on.

She excused herself from the conversation and went to the bathroom to splash water on her face and neck. The slight tint to her cheeks was easily attributed to the weather, as even in March, New Orleans was warm and muggy even after the sun went down. Summer might just kill her.

As she left the bathroom, she found Colin in the narrow hall, leaning against the wall and typing something into his phone. He looked up as she came out.

The awkwardness came back with a vengeance, and she wasn't sure this time how to cover it. "Sorry. I didn't realize there was a line."

His brow wrinkled in confusion, then cleared. "No, I wasn't waiting. I needed a quiet spot to make a phone call and return some emails, and this was the only unoccupied place in the house."

"Oh. Okay." He was obviously busy, so she should go on past. But she didn't know when she'd get another chance. She took a deep breath. "Are you all right with this?"

"With what?"

"Me being here with your friends. Me agreeing to guest blog for Callie. Stuff like that."

Colin shoved his phone back into his pocket and crossed his arms. "I think you overestimate my involvement with Callie's blog, so our interactions with that will be minimal. As for you being here…" He shrugged. "It's a party. Have fun."

"That doesn't really answer my question."

"You're the one who disappeared. Then when you reappeared, you made it clear that you didn't want to have anything to do with me. If anyone's going to have a problem, I'd think it would be you."

That was a little harsh, but true. "I know it sounds clichéd, but it's really not personal. It's not even anything you did—or didn't—do." She was feeling lower than dirt right now, so she dug deep for courage and forged ahead with honesty. "I don't trust myself right now to make good decisions. Especially with men. So I'm being careful. Taking baby steps. Staying in the shallow end."

Colin's eyes roamed down her body in a way that seemed more intimate than a touch. By the time they came back up to her heated face, her breath felt trapped in her chest. "Could've fooled me."

The words could have sounded flip or sneering or dismissive, but the husky edge to Colin's voice made them sound like a caress.

She swallowed hard.

The hallway was dark, the only light coming from the kitchen at the far end. And it was quiet, with the voices outside seeming very far away.

And this was not what she'd expected when she'd decided to open the conversation.

Damn it, she knew what Colin had to be thinking, because she was thinking the same thing. And *knowing* that was somehow worse. Or better. It certainly made the thoughts brighter, clearer...

Colin was still leaning against the wall, but only inches separated them now—which meant she'd been the one moving closer, even though she had no recollection of it. Or even an explanation for it. Without really meaning to, she placed a hand on his chest, and she could feel the heavy thump of his heart through the cotton of his shirt.

This time when she breathed in, she smelled him—

soap and smoke from the grill and something else uniquely Colin that made her thighs clench.

Alarm bells clanged in her head. She needed to heed them this time because this was complicated enough. She stepped back. "Sorry," she managed to choke out.

She had to go.

Colin couldn't move. He could still feel the imprint of her hand on his chest, and the air felt thick and hard to breathe.

Whatever was going on in Jamie's head was complicated and complex, and she was clearly fighting herself. It was small comfort, though, when his zipper was digging into him and his skin was tight.

It took a few minutes to get himself back under control, and when he went back outside and scanned the yard, Jamie was nowhere to be seen. But he did find Callie easily. "Where's Jamie?"

"She left. She said she wasn't feeling well."

He could relate. He felt hot and flushed and his skin felt a size too small.

He hung around a little while longer, but the feeling wouldn't abate. If anything, the edge only grew sharper, honed by frustration. After another twenty minutes, he made his exit, heading home to a cold shower and something stronger than beer.

Dropping his keys and phone on the table by the front door, Colin went straight for the kitchen and the bottle of Jack in the cupboard over the sink. Vetoing the need for a glass, he unscrewed the lid and took a drink. The whiskey was still burning its way down his throat when his doorbell rang.

Everyone he knew was still at Eric's, so he ignored it, only for it to ring again and again a moment later. At least now he could unleash this bad mood on someone who deserved his ire, and he wrenched open the door to do exactly that.

Jamie.

He hadn't thought he was drunk enough—*yet*—to hallucinate. She was backlit by the streetlight, her features shadowed, fingers nervously twisting around themselves. Her lips pressed together as she met his eyes, and Colin's tongue felt too thick to say anything.

It seemed like an age passed before she spoke. "I looked you up and your address is listed. So I came by." She paused and swallowed. "Can I come in?"

He had absolutely no idea what to say, so he nodded and stepped back, opening the door farther for her, and Jamie hesitated for a second before coming in. It was an awkward moment as Jamie closed the door and leaned slightly against it. He waited for her to speak, but when she didn't, he held the bottle in her direction. "Want a drink?"

To his surprise, she nodded, turning the bottle up for a long swallow before grimacing and handing it back. His body felt as though it was vibrating, wanting to touch her, but her silence was unnerving.

Then her hands were on him, wrapping around his neck and pulling his head down to hers as she rose up on tiptoes to meet his mouth.

Pure want hit him with the force of a hurricane, causing him to weave dangerously off balance before righting himself by anchoring his body to hers. Jamie's arms tightened, pulling her into even closer contact as her tongue slipped inside his mouth.

He groaned, wrapping his arms around her waist and deepening the kiss, feeding off her as if he'd been starving for weeks.

Which, in a way, he had.

Jamie's fingers threaded through his hair, holding him, and he caught her sigh in his mouth as she melted against him. Her kiss was hot, wicked and wild, and he trapped her between his body and the wall.

There was no hesitation in her responses, no holding back as she writhed against him, the raw, carnal nature of it completely at odds with the careful distance she'd kept before.

He didn't know what had changed, but he wasn't going to question it too much, either.

And this time, he certainly wasn't going to rush.

He gentled the kiss, running his hands over her cheeks, letting his thumbs stroke her temples and loosening the mass of hair until it fell around her shoulders. Jamie's nails bit into his shoulders in protest as he released her lips and moved down to the soft skin of her neck, slowly and deliberately. With a sigh, her head fell back, giving him better access, and he felt the small shivers of pleasure move over her body as he traced her collarbone with his tongue.

"Colin."

His name was half-sigh, half-groan, escaping from kiss-swollen lips under hooded eyes, and it cut through him like a hot knife, nearly derailing his plan to go slow and savor her.

But if he didn't get her to the bedroom soon, he was going to take her there on the hardwood floor of his foyer without a single regret. As if she were reading his mind, Jamie boosted herself up, wrapping her legs around his waist, and whispered, "Bedroom," in his ear.

He was all too happy to oblige, thankful it wasn't a long walk. In the dim light of his bedroom, he set her carefully on her feet, letting every inch of her body touch his in the process. It was a sweet torture.

One tug and the strapless top of her dress was at her waist. One more and it puddled at her feet, leaving her only in a barely-there thong.

She was even more beautiful than he remembered.

Jamie wasn't sure how much longer her legs were going to hold her upright. Colin didn't even have to touch her—just the heat in his eyes and the long, slow, appreciative looks were turning her muscles to water.

But when he did touch her...

This was what she'd been fighting, what had sent her running from the party, only to find herself a few minutes later sitting on Colin's street watching for him to come home. It hadn't even been a plan, just an inexplicable need.

She knew Colin wanted her, and though she'd tried to fight it, tried to remind herself that she'd be a fool to rush back into anything—much less his arms—the rational, reasonable part of her brain had been shouted down by the sheer force of *want*.

This was probably a mistake, and she might regret it tomorrow, but she didn't care. She had a whole bucket full of unhappy regrets. At least this regret would be a good one.

Colin's hand on her breast caused her breath to catch, only for it to come out a second later in a hiss of pleasure as his thumb rasped over her nipple. He didn't seem to be in a rush, and while the thought of Colin taking his time caused her thighs to clench, she wasn't sure she'd survive the experience.

His shirt joined her dress on the floor, putting that mouthwatering chest on display just for her. For someone who spent most of his time in front of a computer, he was in remarkably good shape, lots of soft skin draped over hard muscle.

She echoed his gesture, tracing her thumb over the ridge of his pectoral muscle, then raking her nail gently over the nipple. Colin's response was swift, grabbing her shoulders and hauling her up for another kiss that scrambled what was left of her mind.

He walked her backward until she felt the mattress against the back of her knees, and she collapsed onto the bed, pulling Colin with her.

Oh, *God*, just the solid weight of him between her thighs was nearly enough to send her over the edge, but Colin just settled and began a leisurely exploration that had her fisting the sheets, unable to take a deep breath.

She cried out when his tongue found her center, arching off the bed as the orgasm went on and on. Before the aftershocks had even abated, Colin was sliding inside, burying himself to the hilt with a groan. *Mercy,* she'd thought these kinds of sensations were a one-off, fueled by the party atmosphere and decadence of Mardi Gras, but she realized that frenzied quickie hadn't even begun to showcase Colin's skills.

Then he kissed her. Equal parts passion and tenderness, that kiss sent tremors through her that she didn't quite understand and couldn't fully process.

But she didn't care. Colin was moving, slowly at first, each stroke seemingly different from the one before, hitting every nerve ending she had—and many she hadn't known she possessed. She was clinging to him, legs wrapped tight around his waist, begging for more.

She could feel the tension building again when Colin began to move faster, and she exploded with a force that scared her, nearly blacking out from the intensity.

The next thing she knew, Colin was stroking her face

and calling her name. It took all the energy she could muster just to open her eyes.

He was just inches above her, sweat glistening on his forehead, a mixture of concern and amusement in his eyes. "You okay?"

She wanted to ask him the same question, as his heart was pounding against her chest at an alarming rate and his breath was uneven, but all she could manage was a tiny nod.

He smiled and dropped his forehead to hers with a sigh. Closing his eyes, he took deep gulping breaths, but one hand kept stroking her from knee to ribs, acting as an anchor for her as she slowly floated back to earth.

Then she heard him chuckle. Opening her eyes again, she found him staring at her. Bracing himself on his elbows, he raised an eyebrow. "*Now* will you tell me your last name?"

She laughed and he grinned at her.

"Vincent. Jamie Vincent."

He dropped a kiss on her forehead. "It's nice to meet you, Jamie Vincent."

CHAPTER SIX

"EXACTLY HOW BIG of a geek are you?"

Jamie mumbled the question against his chest, which she was currently using as a pillow. He looked down, but she didn't move, so he tugged on her hair until she looked up at him. That was a mistake, because her sated, tumbled appearance had an immediate effect on him—which was pretty impressive considering how they'd spent the last couple of hours. He should be mostly dead by now. "Excuse me?"

"I *said,* how big of a geek are you?" She perched her chin on her fist. "Are we talking just a little geeky, or full-out, I've-got-*Star-Trek*-uniforms-in-the-closet geeky?"

"Kirk or Picard?" he shot back, straight-faced.

"Oh, dear Lord."

"Don't worry. They wouldn't fit you anyway." At her shocked look, he rolled her to her back and grinned at her. "My friends got you worried, huh?"

"Not *too* worried, obviously, or I wouldn't be here," she answered primly. "And they were all very nice."

"Yeah, but be warned—some of them *do* have uniforms in their closets." He traced a small circle on her stomach and watched the muscles contract under his fingers. Maybe Jamie wasn't quite worn out yet, either.

"But they were very nice to me, nonetheless."

"You sound surprised."

"Pleased," she corrected. "And appreciative. I've been a little lonely since I moved here." She said it with a sigh.

"What about Kelsey?"

Jamie shook her head. "We're roommates. I answered her room for rent ad online. She's okay as a roommate, but we don't have a lot in common, so…"

She'd mentioned starting over, but it seemed she was trying to start from scratch. "You didn't move here for work and you don't have any friends or family in the area?" She nodded. "Sounds like you're on the run from something."

"Not literally, if that's what you're asking."

Jamie's evasiveness was starting to get on his nerves. This woman-of-mystery crap belonged in movies, not real life. "So why are you here? Now, with me?"

With a sultry look, Jamie ran a finger across his forehead, temple and cheek, ending up at his mouth. "I thought that was pretty self-explanatory."

He waited.

Jamie sighed and pulled the sheet up over her breasts. "I don't have a good answer for that. I wish I did. Does it really matter?"

"Just last week you were insisting that you didn't want anything to do with me." The fact she was here now didn't erase that insult.

"At the time, I thought it would be easier that way. And I wasn't completely wrong, either. It seemed like jumping the gun a little, to get involved with someone when I haven't found my footing yet. Hell, I haven't even found a good dry cleaner yet."

That still didn't answer his question. "So what changed your mind?"

She trailed a hand down his chest and gave him that

smile again. "You're good-looking, charming, smart, great in bed…how could I resist?"

He'd had about enough of this. He rolled off her, out of the bed, and found his jeans. "Jesus, Jamie. If you want to play mind games, find someone else."

"It's not a game. I wish it were, because then there'd be clear rules and I wouldn't have to be figuring it out as I went along." She sat up and watched him as he dressed. "If you didn't want this, you didn't have to let me in to-night."

It was a good thing he was dressed. He probably couldn't have responded naked. "I didn't say I didn't want you, Jamie. In fact, I think I proved that repeatedly."

Exasperated, she threw up her hands. "Then I don't know what you want *from* me."

"You are the strangest person I've ever met. And if you knew the kind of people I normally associate with, you'd realize how high that bar actually is."

"Jeez, you can be such an ass." Jamie rolled off the bed, dragging the sheet behind her. "I thought we could be friends," she muttered.

"Oh, is *that* what this is?"

She turned and fired back, "I don't know. I don't know what I want. I don't know what I'm doing."

"It's not that complicated."

"Maybe not for you," she snapped, grabbing her dress off the floor and stepping into it.

She made no sense at all. "What's *that* supposed to mean?"

She looked him up and down, the muscle in her jaw twitching, before crossing her arms over her chest and leveling a look at him. "You want to know what my deal is? *Fine.* Six weeks ago, I broke off my engage-ment. A five-year engagement. We'd been together since

I was nineteen. That alone should be enough to make me gun shy."

"That doesn't—"

Jamie continued as though he hadn't said anything. "That's bad, of course, but those kinds of things happen to people. But then the bottom really fell out. I'd followed Joey to five different cities over the years supporting his career. Do you know how little of your life is actually *yours* after eight years of that? All my friends were his friends, or the girlfriends of his friends, and none of them joined Team Jamie when we broke up. First I was the fool and then I became the villain. And everything was his—the car, the condo, the furniture. Because we weren't married, I got nothing when I left."

She looked at him expectantly, but he'd been blindsided by this and was still trying to catch up. She snorted and shook her head. "So here I am—no career and no real skills to speak of to get one, no friends. My own sister turned against me. My parents think I'm insane for leaving him. So I had no choice but to find someplace new to start over. And when I say I'm starting over with little more than the clothes on my back, I'm *not* kidding."

He'd wanted to know, but he hadn't expected *that*. Jamie's voice was raw, and he regretted pushing her. And once again, he didn't know what to say. "That does sound bad."

Jamie's eyes widened and he was now regretting saying anything at all. "Ya think?" she snapped. "So, yeah, I'm feeling a little crazy right now. I'm also freaked out and more than a bit scared. And so, no, I don't have a damn clue what I'm doing here with you."

She ran her hands through her hair and seemed to give herself a good shake. With another one of those ex-

asperated sighs, she turned her back on him and walked
out the door.

And now he felt like a total ass.

Jamie felt shaky inside. She hadn't meant to say any of
that—much less *all* of that. At the same time, she hadn't
realized how close to the surface it all was, nor how ten-
der she would be to someone poking her about it. But
she'd said it, so she'd own it, and she'd walk out of there
with her head held high. Giving in to her mysterious attraction to Colin had been a big mistake.

She should have heeded the signs from the get-go and
not let her hormones take over.

But now it would be out of her system, and she'd plan
on keeping her distance from him from this point on.

Her shoes were in the hall, keys and purse in the foyer
where she'd dropped them when she'd launched herself
at Colin. She had her hand on the door when she heard
him speak from behind her.

"R.J.'s Quality Cleaners on Canal."

She spun around to see Colin leaning against the door
frame to his bedroom. *"What?"*

"A good dry cleaner. They're fast, reasonably priced
and they do a good job. I've known the family for years."

She couldn't really process that information. It *seemed*
as if it should make sense, yet at the same time it didn't.

"You said you needed to find a dry cleaner." He
walked toward her, a small smile teasing the corner of
his mouth. "Well, that's now one thing you can scratch
off your list."

"Thank you." She didn't really know what else to say
to that.

"If you need money," he continued, "I'm sure Teddy
would let you pick up some shifts at the Lucky Gator.

It's probably not the career you're looking for, but it'd be quick cash to cover the rent at least while you look."

What is he doing? She didn't realize she'd said it aloud until he answered her.

"Trying to help."

This was why she shouldn't overshare. "I don't want pity."

"It's not pity. You said you thought we could be friends. Friends help each other out."

A little glow of hope lit in her chest. She'd been telling herself all the right things, but she realized now that she didn't quite believe her own pep talks. Somehow, this overture—as weird and unexpected as it was—helped her believe.

"Thank you," she said again, but this time she meant it.

"It's true you've got a lot on your plate, but don't panic over it. Embrace it. You can't start over just to spite your past."

His voice was soothing and slightly hypnotic, and it didn't help that he was still shirtless, mussed and delicious-looking. She still had too many post-orgasmic endorphins rocketing through her bloodstream for *that* to go unnoticed by her libido. Being friendly or not, part of her recognized that he was clearly trying to woo her back to bed, and damn it, it was working. She wasn't going to address his last comment, because that might lead to more oversharing, and there was still an awful lot of that she needed to sort out for herself before she started taking advice from others. But the other thing he'd said... "I wouldn't mind having a friend."

He smiled at her, and while she returned it, the moment felt a little heavier than she'd have liked or wanted to think about. "We don't have much in common," she warned. "My laptop is strictly for surfing and shopping, and I've never seen *Star Wars*."

"That's a pity, but I have other friends for that." He held out his hand, palm up.

Jamie hesitated for a moment, part of her thinking it wasn't such a bright idea, but another part of her shouting that it was, for all kinds of reasons. It was a little confusing, but in the end, it came down to two things: she liked Colin, and the occasional brain-scrambling roll in the sack would be good for her overall mental health.

Not to mention very satisfying.

She put her hand in his and his fingers closed around it. There was an exhilarating rush of excitement as her body shifted into gear, expectation shimmering through her insides.

But there was something else, too. Something she didn't want to investigate too closely.

But that was okay. She'd just take everything one step at a time.

And the first step was back toward Colin's bed.

The sky was beginning to lighten as she quietly closed the door behind her. She was exhausted, bleary eyed and not fully steady on her feet. Colin had grumbled when she got up to get dressed, coaxing her to come back to bed, to sleep a little while longer.

Thankfully, he'd fallen back asleep quickly, his breaths slow, deep and even.

That was a good thing, because she wouldn't have been able to give good reasons why she wouldn't—or actually couldn't—stay. How was she supposed to articulate the fact that spending the night, the whole night—and actually *sleeping* with him, much less waking up with him—would put her in very uncomfortable territory?

It seemed smarter and safer to not go there quite yet, hence her stealthy exit.

Dark stubble had lined Colin's chin, and his hair stuck up at crazy angles. He, though, had still looked scrumptious in ways that nearly had her crawling back under the covers with him. She couldn't say the same for herself, as the image that greeted her in the rearview mirror was downright scary.

Anyone who saw her would know exactly how she'd spent the night.

But she couldn't really bring herself to regret it. She felt calmer than she had in weeks, more relaxed and sure of herself. Maybe there really was something to that whole you-just-need-to-get-laid thing.

She still wasn't convinced that getting involved with someone was a good idea at this point, and she'd never had sex with a man she hadn't been in a committed relationship with. She'd heard of friends with benefits before, and wondered if it could possibly be that easy.

It would certainly be nice.

"It was so cool. You just don't appreciate the level of detail that goes into them until you see it up close. And they're *huge*." Jamie sat cross-legged on his living room floor, the pizza in front of her gone cold as she bubbled over, sharing every detail she'd learned on her tour about how parade floats were made.

He laughed. "So you've told me. Six times."

Jamie made a face at him. "I'm sorry I'm not as jaded about the whole thing as you are. *I* still find it very interesting and exciting."

"You know, I've lived here my entire life and I've never been to Mardi Gras World."

Her jaw dropped. "You're kidding."

"Nope."

She grabbed the brochure she'd brought back with her. "There's a VIP tour that's like twenty bucks extra, and I'm really thinking about going back to do that. You could come with me when I do."

"I'll pass, thanks. Anyway," he pushed to his feet and went to the kitchen for a refill, "I thought you were busy job hunting, not sightseeing."

"I'm doing both, thank you very much. I sent in three more résumés this morning before I went on my tour. In the meantime, I took your advice and got a job waiting tables in the interim. I start day after tomorrow." She grinned as she finally picked up her pizza and took a bite.

"Good for you." He sat next to her on the floor and leaned against the couch. "I happen to know for a fact that the money at the Lucky Gator is pretty good."

She shook her head as she swallowed. "Not the Gator. It's a place called Beauregard's."

He nearly choked on his drink. *Sweet God.* "Beauregard's is kind of rough, don't you think?"

She waved that away. "It's fine."

"No, it's not. Didn't someone get stabbed in the parking lot a couple of weeks ago?"

"And things like that *never* happen in the Quarter, of course," she said, rolling her eyes.

"But I know Teddy would look out for you."

"I don't need Teddy to look out for me." At his look, she sighed. "Fine. I promise I won't hang out in the parking lot, okay? The servers make good money there, and it's close to my place. That's all I really care about at the moment."

"Teddy would give you a job, you know."

"I know. But I don't want to work at the Lucky Gator."

"Why not?"

"Because."

That wasn't a good answer. "Because *why?*"

Exasperated, Jamie tossed the rest of her slice back into the box. "Because Teddy is a friend of yours, and I wanted to see if I could get a job on my own."

"And now that you know you can—"

"I'm going to keep it," she interrupted, leveling a hard look at him.

He shrugged. "I'm just trying to help."

"And it's appreciated, but unnecessary. I'm a big girl, Colin." She wiped her fingers on a napkin, then crawled across the floor to straddle his lap. "I know you mean well, and it's very sweet—if also a little annoying," she warned. "But I've got to do this on my own. It's important to me."

"It would be easier, though, if you'd just—"

She put a finger over his lips. "Subject closed. Now, I'm going to the Backstreet Cultural Museum in Tremé tomorrow. Want to come with me?"

"I thought you went there already."

"No, I was going to, but I went to the Presbytere instead. They have a fantastic Mardi Gras exhibit, but Backstreet is supposed to go deeper into the cultural aspects and African-American influence on Mardi Gras."

He settled his hands on her hips and adjusted her so he still kept circulation to his legs. "You know, there's so much more to New Orleans than just Mardi Gras. We do manage to entertain ourselves the other ten months of the year."

She grinned. "But I *like* Mardi Gras."

"So do I. But there's music and food and all kinds of history and...well, things that *aren't* Mardi Gras."

"I know. I bought the guidebook, Colin."

"I'm talking about the things that aren't in the guidebooks. The places the tourists don't really know about. You're a local now, so you should experience what New Orleans is really like."

"I'm not really a local yet."

"But you don't want to live like a tourist forever, do you? Let me take you out and show you the real New Orleans. *My* New Orleans. The clubs, the restaurants…all the reasons I love this city."

Her head tilted to one side. "Like on an actual date?"

He hadn't really thought of it like that. He and Jamie had been spending a lot of time together this week, but it was mostly in bed. He knew every inch of her body, every way to make her whimper and scream, but they hadn't had what anyone could call a date. It sounded a bit like backtracking at this point, but… "Yeah. Like a date."

She slid off his lap. "I'm not sure I'm ready for that."

He had to wonder about Jamie's ex, what he'd done to her to not only send her running off to a new city but to also have her build such solid walls around herself. She never talked about her past except in very vague terms, but then she never asked about his past, either, thank God. He didn't want to get all confessional about his life and his family, so he couldn't get too upset over *her* avoidance of the same kind of topics.

So it was a rather weird arrangement, being both more *and* less than friends. She'd come to his house, they'd have amazing, hanging-from-the-chandeliers sex, but she wouldn't stay the night, always heading home once the afterglow faded. And while they talked about everything from pop culture to politics, they simply didn't delve too deeply into personal topics. It was either very healthy or very sick, and the sad part was that he didn't know which.

"It's dinner, not a marriage proposal, Jamie."

"I know, and it seems silly, considering..." She sighed. "Sure. It'll be fun."

Boy, Jamie was tough on his ego. "Your enthusiasm is simply overwhelming."

"It's not a lack of enthusiasm. It's just strange. I mean, I had a plan for moving here. Get a job, maybe a cat, get my head screwed on straight.... Dating wasn't really part of that plan."

"But celibacy was?"

She shrugged. "Kind of. I mean, why complicate life unnecessarily?"

"But..."

"But here I am with you. And I'm not saying that's a bad thing," she added quickly, "just unexpected. Hell, I'm already giving advice to other people about their love lives, and if that's not the most ironic and ridiculous thing ever, I don't know what is."

"I've read your first *Ex Factor* column. It didn't seem ridiculous to me."

"Really?"

He nodded.

She elbowed him. "And? Did you like it? Is it okay?"

"Fishing for compliments?"

"No. I'm simply worried I'm going to screw this up right out of the gate."

He rubbed her leg. "I thought it was great. Insightful and amusing at the same time."

"Really?" She looked both earnest and pleased at the same time. "You wouldn't lie to me to make me feel better?"

"Nope."

She blew out her breath. "Good, because I don't want to let Callie down. She barely knows me and she's letting me fill in for her."

They were a bit far afield from the earlier topic of going out, but this seemed important to her, so he went with it. Maybe relieving *that* worry might bring her around, too. "Even if it wasn't good—which it is, so stop worrying—Callie isn't going to hate you for it. It's just a little advice column."

"And it's a little scary, because I'm not sure I should be giving advice about other people's love lives and problems, considering my own past."

He couldn't consider her past or her ex, but there was no sense mentioning that. "These are people who write to strangers for advice. *Anonymous* strangers who do not even pretend to have any education or training to back up that advice. It would be kind of hard to screw that up."

"Callie's not anonymous on the site."

"True. They know they're asking an unmarried wedding planner and her ex-boyfriend for relationship tips. That's messed up in ways I can't even describe."

"Yet you do it anyway."

"As a favor to Callie."

Casually, almost too casually, Jamie said, "Callie's great. I like her."

"Good."

"Should that be weird?"

"What do you mean?"

"Callie's your ex, and we are…" She fumbled for words. "Well, we are *this*."

Well, that was an enlightening description. "Callie and I haven't been a couple since our freshman year in college. Any weirdness is long past."

"But you still care about her."

"Of course. We're friends."

"Yeah, but so are *we*, and…" She looked at him evenly.

"Look, if there's something going on between you two, I really don't want to get in the middle of it and mess it up."

"If you're asking if I'm still in love with her, the answer is no. If you're asking if we still sleep together occasionally, the answer is also no. We're not *that* kind of friends."

Jamie nodded without lifting her eyes from her hands. "Can I ask how long it took for you to get over her?"

"What?"

"Y'all were obviously together for a while."

"A couple of years. But we were kids."

"What broke you up?"

"A lot of things." When Jamie didn't say anything, he sighed. "Didn't you ask Callie? I thought y'all were friends now." This seemed exactly like the kind of things girls would dish about, and that actually made him a little uncomfortable, now that he thought about it.

"Not like close friends. She just said y'all dated in high school and left it at that. I didn't want to pry."

"But you'll ask me about it?"

"Yeah." When he didn't say anything, she nudged him with her foot. "Come on. What happened? I'm curious. Did you cheat on her?"

There was something in her voice that told him more about her ex than she probably intended. "No, of course not."

"Then what?"

"You're not going to let this go, are you?"

She shook her head.

He sighed. *So much for not prying into the past.* "Callie went away for college—"

"Which hurt your feelings?"

"Maybe. In a way. She could have stayed local, but

she got a scholarship to Wimbly Southern and took it. She changed while she was gone."

"People do that when they go away to college."

"I was only eighteen, remember? I didn't have any type of perspective on life. All I knew was that my girlfriend chose to go away, became a totally different person, and then I had to go save her ass when she got into trouble. We had a huge fight, and I was going into my exams, and I nearly flunked them all that semester. And since I wasn't on a scholarship like she was, I knew I couldn't afford to retake the classes. Things went downhill from there pretty quickly."

"So it was her fault?"

That was a tricky question, not that Jamie had any reason to think so. He'd blamed Callie at the time, but he had perspective now. He'd driven all the way to Mississippi to bail her out of jail, only to get blasted by her, as she did not want nor need his help. The long, miserable drive back had been bad enough, only to arrive home to find that his mother had been taken to the hospital in a nearly psychotic rage. That episode had been bad enough to finally get his mother officially diagnosed and medicated, but the guilt of his trip pushing her to that edge and his anger and misery over his fight with Callie had nearly derailed his exams. It had taken him awhile to put the pieces back together that time. Callie had been more the catalyst than the cause, so he couldn't lay all the blame on her. At least not now.

He looked sideways at Jamie, who seemed to be patiently awaiting his answer. He might not want to share, but he didn't want to lie, either. "Not entirely, but that was the last straw. For both of us, but for different reasons."

"But you're friends now. And you write *The Ex Factor* together."

"That took a while, though. We lived in the same town, we had a lot of the same friends.... It wasn't like we could cut each other out of our lives completely."

"But you didn't get back together."

"Young love is great, but it doesn't have staying power."

Jamie's mouth twisted and he remembered her saying something about meeting her ex when she was nineteen. *Oops.* At the same time, she was proof he was right. "And *The Ex Factor?*"

"*The Ex Factor* was kind of an accident. I built her website for her a few years ago, and one day I noticed she had written her take on a recent celebrity breakup. To this day I don't know why, but I responded. People loved it and it became a thing."

"That's nice." Jamie stared at her hands again.

"So is this really about Callie, or is it about *your* ex?" This time he had to nudge her when she didn't answer.

She made a noise between a snort and a laugh. "I don't see me and Joey being friends in the future. We're not kids, and this isn't kid stuff. There's a bit more dirt and disaster going on."

He shouldn't be pressing this. He'd be a hypocrite to do so when he'd been almost as vague about him and Callie and their breakup. But there was one thing he did want to know—and it was fair game since she'd started it. "Are you still in love with him?"

"No. And I don't want him back, either." She answered quickly and adamantly—almost *too* quickly and adamantly. As if she might be trying to convince herself as well as him. "I certainly can't forgive him. But he was a part of my life for a long time, so..." She shrugged. "It's weird."

"Life is weird."

"That it is." And with that, her wall went back up, clearly bringing that topic to an end.

"Any more questions about Callie?"

"Nope."

"Good. Because I'd really rather not think about Callie right now."

"Oh, why is that?"

"Because otherwise it would be a little disturbing when I did *this*." He hauled Jamie back into his lap and kissed her. He didn't want to shine flashlights into dark places in either of their pasts. Nothing good could come of it. Sometimes you just had to let the circus pack its tents and move on for a while. God knew it would come back to town eventually, so why revisit when it wasn't absolutely necessary?

Her arms went around his neck without hesitation, massaging the nape as she melted into him. She hummed as his fingers massaged her thighs, and he found that place on the side of her neck that she liked. "This is very nice."

"Mmm-hmm," he answered, slipping his hands under her shirt to release the clasp of her bra.

They didn't even make it to the bedroom.

CHAPTER SEVEN

You can come home. He misses you. We all do.
We're worried about you.

JAMIE SAT ON the back deck of Beauregard's, eating her free post-shift meal as she stared at her phone and the unexpected message. She wasn't sure how to respond to that. She'd once considered Michelle a friend, but Michelle had been one of the first to cut her out as soon as her loyalty to Joey wavered even the tiniest bit, and she'd found out they actually weren't friends after all. This message had come straight out of nowhere.

Hell, she wasn't even sure if she should respond at all.

She'd admit—but only to herself—that she'd toyed with the idea of going back. This was much harder than she'd expected it to be. Waitressing was keeping her afloat for the time being, but she didn't enjoy it, she wasn't very good at it and nothing better seemed to be coming along, no matter how many résumés she sent out.

She'd met some people at work, made a few friends—not besties, but folks she could hang out with, at least. She wasn't getting horribly lost every time she set foot outside anymore, and she was even starting to understand the local accents and idioms. The other day she'd discovered her tire was flat and managed to deal with it all by herself. Okay, not totally by herself; she'd knocked on the neighbor's door and paid him fifteen dollars to help her. But she'd paid very close attention and was pretty sure she'd be able to change it herself next time.

For the first time in her life, she felt like a fully-functioning adult member of society.

She didn't necessarily *like* it all the time—things like insurance were just a pain in the butt—but by God, she was doing it. It wasn't anything like her old life, but she was proving Joey and everyone else a little more wrong each day.

But it was still tempting. Oh, so tempting.

It was like quitting smoking: every day that she didn't give in to the temptation was a little victory. She just needed to hold onto her pride.

Taking a deep breath, she quickly typed, Tell everyone I'm fine. But I'm not coming back.

She hit send before she could lose her nerve.

Almost immediately, like a message from the universe that she'd done the right thing, another message pinged to her phone, this time from Colin: Are you coming over tonight?

Colin was possibly the only thing keeping her sane at the moment, but even that had its own caution lights. She liked him—a lot—but she had to question whether it was smart to get too attached to him. She was well aware of the dangers of rebounding—especially coming off a relationship like hers—and she didn't want to cling to him for all the wrong reasons.

It was getting harder to keep him at arm's length, though; there were moments when she almost said too much, and times when she wanted to say more. But she could tell he was keeping his distance, too. Too many silences, too many conversational curves. She knew what *she* wasn't willing to talk about, but she had to wonder what topics he was intentionally avoiding and why.

Not that she could really ask unless she was ready to spill her own guts as well.

Mercy. She had to question how healthy this really was for her....

But her body was already on board, a lovely anticipatory glow crawling up from her toes at the mere thought. It was hard to fight.

I can't. Working tonight.

Come by after?

What did Colin think she was? Just some kind of a booty call? Other plans made already, she typed. That wasn't entirely false; a couple of the other waitresses had been after her to go out for a drink after work for a while now. It was time she took them up on it.

A few minutes later, Colin's response came back: Okay. See you later.

Damn it, she'd kill to know the tone behind that. Disappointed? Perfectly fine? Peeved? She was certainly feeling something like disappointment, but it was hard to track where it stemmed from. Was she hoping that he'd try a little harder to convince her? Or should she be glad that he hadn't?

It was all very confusing.

Welcome to my life. Was there anything in it that *wasn't* confusing?

With a sigh, she cleared her table and clocked back in for her next shift. And while she tried to be perky for the sake of her customers, that confused feeling stayed with her all night.

Figuring she would have to learn to trust herself eventually, she left the restaurant at the end of her shift and found herself at Colin's door a few minutes later.

He seemed surprised to see her. "I thought you had other plans tonight."

"I sort of did. But I decided I'd rather be with you." It felt good to say that out loud. And she meant it.

He grinned and pulled her inside.

"So *why* are we killing the zombies again?"

"Because they're zombies and this is the zombie apocalypse. They're the bad guys," Colin explained.

Jamie was seated next to him on the bed, wearing nothing but one of his old T-shirts, his laptop in her lap and a mouse on a book beside her, her forehead wrinkled as she stared at the screen, where zombies shuffled down Bourbon Street. A half-naked girl, a bottle of wine and a computer game in his bed at the same time had to rate high on any geek's ultimate wish list, but he wasn't entirely sure why he'd agreed to appease her curiosity about *No Quarter* at three in the morning instead of finding something better to occupy them. In fact, he'd never been less interested in a game in his life than he was at this moment.

"Isn't zombie killing more of a job for law enforcement?" she asked. "Or maybe the military? I mean, they have much better weapons than just a baseball bat."

"Well, you can earn better weapons, and the military isn't going to help—"

"Wait," she interrupted, "so you're telling me there's no military after the zombie apocalypse? Has our entire system of government collapsed as well?"

"Well…" He started to try to explain, realized he couldn't, and just said, "They're busy somewhere else."

"In that case, then maybe it would be smarter to just hole up indoors and wait?" Jamie gestured at the screen, where a zombie had just tripped and fallen. "I mean, they're zombies, not a pack of Einsteins. A good lock should stymie them until help arrives."

"That rather defeats the entire purpose of the game."

She shot a sideways glance at him, then frowned at the screen again. "Well, I'm not sure I'm sold on that whole purpose anyway."

He let that slide. "Now, your mouse lets you look around—"

"Whoa, motion sickness much?" She moved the mouse slowly this time, turning her avatar in a circle to see her surroundings. "This is amazing, Colin. You really designed all of this yourself?"

"Well, Eric, too. And a few other folks. It started off as a project we played with when we were still in high school—only back then it was aliens invading—and then we expanded on it while we were in college. We were studying programming, so we'd apply what we learned to the game. Eventually we changed the aliens to zombies and invited others to play. It got popular and grew from there, and we've been playing catch-up ever since."

"But making this…I just can't imagine. Not just the programming either, but also the concept, the story, all of it." She grinned at him. "You are really smart. Like genius smart."

There was just enough surprise in her voice to tell him that she'd never given games a thought before, but there was also an admiration that wasn't at all faked. It was quite flattering. "Maybe not genius…"

"Well, you're definitely the smartest guy I've ever been with." Then she pointed to the avatars in the upper corner of her screen. "Who are all of those people?"

Now he was both pleased he'd showed her the game and still regretting it at the same time. His brain was having a hard time holding both emotions simultaneously. "They are the other players currently online."

"I'm supposed to play with other people?"

"If you want. You don't have to, but it's called a massively *multi*player online game for a reason."

"Oh, okay." She cracked her knuckles. "Let's do this. Who goes first?"

"No one goes first. It's not that kind of game. If you joined them, you'd work together as a team to fight the zombies."

She looked at him strangely. "So how do you win this game, then?"

"You don't. You can accomplish your objectives, secure areas and complete missions, but the game itself never ends. There are always more zombies."

Jamie rolled her eyes. "Well, that's just ridiculous. What's the point?"

He'd never thought about it. That's just how it was. "The point of games isn't necessarily to win."

"Actually, it is. That's why they're called games."

"The fun is in the *playing*," he stressed.

"And in the *winning*," she stressed just as earnestly.

"Look, people pay me money to play this game. I *want* them to continue playing indefinitely."

"Okay, *that* makes sense." She leaned back and reached for her drink. "I'll confess I don't really see the attraction, though."

"You're not my target audience."

"Very true." She moved the laptop to the floor, giving him a lovely view of her thighs and butt, before flopping back on the pillows with a dramatic sigh. "How is that satisfying, though? An unending catastrophe and no way to ever win? We get enough of that in real life, thanks very much. The zombies are just added suckitude."

"Oh, but there is satisfaction. You clear an area, secure it against future attacks…"

"But the zombies keep coming."

He shrugged. "I get great satisfaction from killing zombies."

"I think I'd prefer something where I had a bit more control. I've got enough uncontrollable stuff in my real life, thanks very much."

"Ah, but you forget—I *do* have control. It's my game. I made it." He rolled to his back, arms spread wide. "I am the ultimate supreme power in that universe," he declared in his best supervillain voice, throwing in an evil laugh for good measure. "Even the zombies bend to my will."

"Somebody's on a power trip."

He wasn't going to deny it. That power was what had attracted him to games in the first place. No matter how crazy things got with his mother, he could always lose himself in a game where the bad guys were obvious and bested by skill. Even the most complicated-seeming games were nothing but code and scripted actions, predictable and constant. It didn't take a psychology degree to figure out that he had started building worlds where he was God in response to the fact that the real world was way out of his control. Hell, he freely admitted it. He turned his head to grin at Jamie. "Jealous?"

"Of someone who has ultimate godlike powers over the fates of thousands of people's virtual lives? *Absolutely.* I'd love that kind of control."

"Oh, really?"

"Yep." In a flash, she'd straddled him, knees braced on either side of his hips. She put her hands on his biceps, gently pinning him to the mattress. "Not only would I love it, I'd totally get off on it," she purred, leaning down to press her lips to his chest. In slow, tantalizing movements, Jamie brushed her breasts across his torso, letting him feel hard nipples covered only in thin cotton. Her hips rocked gently back against his groin, teasing him and causing him to buck in response.

A slow, sexy smile spread across Jamie's face, and she released the pressure on his arms long enough to sweep the T-shirt she wore up and off. Then she reached for his arms and pressed them up over his head.

She was getting off on the control, but then so was he. She slid up his body, letting him feel every inch of her skin, and brushed a nipple across his lips. "I'd be a benevolent ruler, you know. Keep everyone happy. I'd get rid of the zombies, the violence, and make it Mardi Gras in the Quarter all the time. Just music and parades and this." She brushed the other nipple across his lips but pulled back when he tried to capture it, sliding back down to press a hot kiss against his neck.

"You want the power?" She lifted her head. "The total control?" He waited for her nod, then flipped her to her back, reversing their positions and capturing her wrists in his hands above her head. Jamie's mouth opened in a little O of shock. "Design your own game. The zombies stay."

Jamie stuck out her tongue and he kissed her long and hard. She sighed into his mouth. And though he released her wrists to free his hands for another exploration of that creamy skin, she kept them where they were, wrapping her fingers around the slats of his headboard.

Shortly thereafter, Jamie began to whimper, arching against his hands and mouth. A few minutes later, she was screaming his name.

As he moved over her again, she released the headboard and raked her fingers through his hair. "I may have been wrong earlier."

"About what?"

"There's quite a bit of fun in the playing, too."

Two days later, they actually went out for the first time. Colin rang the doorbell to her apartment, and when Jamie opened the door, his tongue nearly hit his shoes. A silky red dress hugged her curves, managing to show both generous cleavage and leg, and offset her creamy skin. Oh, it begged to be peeled off of her. Her hair was pulled up again in a complicated sexy twist off her neck, and her eyes were darkly lined and smoky. "I…you…um…"

Jamie grinned. "I'll take that as a compliment. And you look very 'I…you…um…' as well." She grabbed a wrap and a tiny purse, but then paused. "I hope this is okay. I've never been to a real jazz club before."

Damn him and his stupid idea to take her out. He had to search to find his voice. "It's perfect. I'll be the envy of every guy in the place."

She rose up on her tiptoes to give him a kiss. "Flattery will get you everywhere."

The club wasn't far and the air not too muggy tonight, so they walked. They'd only gone a block when Jamie slid her hand into his. "So how are things in the Dungeons today?"

"Pretty exciting, actually."

"Troll uprising?" she teased.

"Not exactly.

She looked at him sideways. "Will I have a clue what you're talking about if I ask what?"

"Maybe. I just signed a very lucrative contract today to license the engine we built for the new game."

"I doubt engine means what I think it means, but licensing I do understand. That's awesome. Especially if it's lucrative." She squeezed his hand and pulled his arm in close to her. "I'm glad we're going out tonight. We can celebrate."

"You are in an awfully good mood."

She shot him a look of mock offense. "Are you saying I'm not always a glorious ray of sunshine?"

"I'm just saying you're sunnier than usual."

"It's because I *am* in a good mood. I think I'm at a tipping point."

"For...?"

"It just feels like things are starting to settle—in a good way. That stuff I wrote for Callie's blog is getting tons of hits and great comments, so my ego's getting a bit of a stroking right now. *And* I got a callback for a second interview at a place I'm really excited about."

"That's great. Where?"

"Roth and Howe. They're an interior design firm and their work is simply *beautiful*. It's just a receptionist and general office job right now, but design and decor are really up my alley and there's a chance for advancement down the road." Jamie sounded giddy. "So think good thoughts for me Friday, okay?"

He could do more than that. He'd gone to school with Kate Roth. She'd overseen all of the renovations to Rainstorm's offices, and he'd done troubleshooting on her computers when she'd first started her business. He'd send her an email later tonight. "My fingers are crossed."

"So I've had a great couple of days, I'm really optimistic about the future, and I'm out for a fabulous night with a really great guy. My life does not suck right now."

"I'm glad to hear it."

The club was only a few steps away, and the music floated out the open door. Jamie stopped and pulled him aside. "I know we got a weird start and I've been all over the place mentally, but you put up with me and I appreciate that."

He ran a hand down the soft skin of her arm. "It wasn't purely altruistic on my part, you know."

Jamie toyed with the lapel of his jacket and looked up at him through her eyelashes. "Good." Then her hand tightened and she pulled him close for a kiss that, once again, had him regretting they'd left the house.

He groaned and broke the kiss. "Careful," he murmured against her lips, "or else we're going to end up in that alley doing something that will get us arrested."

"I'm almost willing to risk it."

Pressing her against the wall, he let Jamie feel exactly what she was doing to him. "We can go home, you know…"

"No. We're going to go into this club, have a couple of drinks, possibly even a dance…"

The thought of Jamie pressed against him in a slow sway made him light-headed as all the blood in his body rushed south. He dropped his forehead to hers and groaned.

Jamie straightened his collar. "And *then* we'll go back to your place and…" She trailed off as another couple passed by, then whispered her ideas into his ear. With a cheeky grin, she slipped out from under his arms and dragged him toward the club's doors. "Come on. I could use a drink."

So could I.

She was going to drive him crazy.

And he was looking forward to it.

Jamie didn't even try to hide her distaste as Colin handed her a slimy raw oyster that jiggled nastily in its shell. "I'm not eating that."

Even if she managed to swallow the gross-looking thing and it somehow stayed down, it seemed like an excellent way to get food poisoning. This restaurant—and she used the term loosely, at best—looked ready to be shut down by the health department at any moment. Colin might have wanted to show her the real New Orleans, but she'd had visions of interesting little cafés or jazz clubs like the one they went to the other night, not dive bars where the music was nearly deafening and the sanitation questionable.

Colin arched an eyebrow at her. "You just talked me into spending more money on a suit than I spent on my first car. You can now eat a raw oyster."

"That suit is unbelievably sexy and looks like a million bucks on you. That oyster," she pushed the offering away, "is gross and looks like you scraped it off the sidewalk out front. No, thank you."

"Sexy and a million bucks, huh?" he said with a grin as he tipped up the shell and let the oyster slide in his mouth.

She repressed the shudder creeping up her spine. "One of the few things I know about in this world is fashion. That suit is worth every penny you paid for it. And you're a grown man, for goodness' sake. You should own a decent suit."

"I don't like ties."

"I told you, then don't wear one. Wear the gray shirt and leave the collar unbuttoned. You'll be the sexiest geek ever at your launch party."

"Thanks, but I don't think that crowd will really appreciate a sexy factor."

"Sounds like a crap party, then," she teased.

"That it will be," he grumbled into his glass.

"Hey, I was kidding." The server brought her food and

she was glad to find that the oysters hadn't killed her appetite completely.

"I'm not. It's really just a media thing. Show off the game, answer questions, talk it all up for the bloggers and gaming websites. I'm dreading it."

"Well, with that attitude…"

"You'll come, right?"

She laughed around her bite of hushpuppy. "Hmm, a half-assed invite to a crap party? I'll pass."

"It won't be too boring for you. I know for a fact the food will be good, and there will be a couple of celebs who did the voice work for the game there for you to meet."

Jamie realized Colin was serious with his invitation. She'd smiled her way through plenty of press events before, but she'd figured that part of her life was behind her now. Not that there'd be a lot of crossover between the gaming press and the sports press—or probably their audiences—but she still didn't want to show up on a blog again so soon. However accidentally or tangentially. But how to turn him down? "I think I'd be more of a liability than anything else in that setting. I don't know the first thing about games. Or dungeons or dragons or trolls, for that matter."

"You don't need to. You could just smile and look pretty."

Ugh. She kept her eyes on her food, waiting for her eyelid to quit twitching. "Um…"

But Colin seemed to be warming to the subject. "I could be king of the geeks, showing up in a swanky suit with a beautiful woman on my arm." He winked at her. "I bet you'd make great arm candy."

Her stomach actually rolled over at the phrase. "Do

you have any idea how insulting that term is?" she snapped.

Colin pulled back at the heat in her voice. "Sorry."

Damn it. "Anyway, this is a big night for you. Isn't there someone else you'd rather have there?"

"It's my party, Jamie. I control the guest list."

"I realize that."

He put a hand over hers. "And I'd really like for you to come."

Something shifted, making this invitation seem more important than she'd initially thought. Going to his launch party was a big step, far more so than going on dates or even sleeping with him. It moved things forward in a way that kind of scared her a bit. But she couldn't turn him down flat, either. It would be insulting, possibly hurtful, and although she didn't want to be his arm candy—*ugh*—or get anywhere near the press again, the need to make him happy seemed more important. Damn, she did not like being forced to make a decision like this on the spot. "I'll have to see if I can get off work," she hedged, stalling for time to really think about it.

But Colin seemed to accept that as a yes, and kissed her before turning back to his oysters.

"Okay, this game was way overhyped," Eric complained as they sat across from each other in the Rainstorm conference room, each of them at a laptop as they played through a couple of levels on a game just released by another company—strictly for research purposes, of course.

"And buggy." Colin swore and hit the keyboard a little harder than normal. "Damn, this thing lags like hell. And the interface sucks."

"Agreed. Hey, dude, you're shooting at me."

"Not intentionally."

Eric sighed. "This is so sad. I'm stuck in a room with you at nine o'clock on a Friday night shooting at aliens. I've *got* to get myself a woman."

He looked at Eric over the top of his screen. "Got to get yourself a woman? You sound like you're fourteen years old."

"Emotionally, I probably am," Eric deadpanned.

Colin nodded as the game stuttered again. "At least you know the root of the problem. That's the first step."

"So I know why I'm here. Why aren't you with Jamie?"

"She had to work. I think she's coming over later."

"Things are getting serious between you, then."

"What?" They'd been together only a couple of weeks. It couldn't be remotely classified as serious.

"I mean, you're certainly spending a lot of time with her."

"Jealous?" Colin shook his head and sighed, closing out the game. "I give up on this. It sucks."

"I admit I'm a little jealous. I mean, you have to be the only man in the history of the world who picks up a girl in the French Quarter on Mardi Gras for a drunken hookup and it *doesn't* turn out to be a cautionary tale."

It wasn't exactly a fairy tale, either. Sometimes he felt as though they were in a holding pattern. "I'm just lucky, I guess."

"Damn lucky. I know if I tried that, I'd end up with a bunny-boiling psycho. Or a cult member who needed a sacrifice."

He was pretty sure Jamie didn't fall into either of those categories. *But...* "Don't be so dramatic."

"Just because the girl you found is gorgeous and nor-mal and sane, that's no reason for me to think that I could repeat that miracle." He heard Eric's laptop shutting down as he closed the top. "Unless there's a flaw in the peach you're not telling me about."

"Nope, sorry."

Eric sighed. "I knew that would be too much to hope for."

"Whoa, some kind of friend you are."

"Well, she did jerk you around some at the beginning. I can take a bit of satisfaction from that. What brought about the big change in attitude?"

That was actually a very good question. He hadn't wanted to question his good luck, though, choosing to avoid thinking about it too much instead. But that was getting harder to do. "I guess my charm was just too irresistible for her to overcome."

"You wish. Although if you do ever figure it out, we could make a fortune selling that secret to men everywhere. We'd be able to retire."

Colin's phone pinged, and a message from Jamie appeared on his screen: About to leave work. Headed to your place. "And that's my cue to leave, because I have a life."

"Must be nice," Eric grumbled before brightening up. "Hey, ask Jamie if she has a friend, will you? Someone normal who might be interested in a smart, successful entrepreneur who owns his own business—"

"Co-owns," he corrected.

"Fine, co-owns," Eric amended. "But ask her, okay?"

"I'll ask, but it would probably be one of the women she works with. Jamie hasn't had a chance to make a lot of friends yet."

"No wonder she's latched onto you, then. The poor girl is lonely."

Colin put his hand to his heart in mock distress. "Wow,

the support in this room is just amazing. I feel all tingly from it."

"Smart-ass. I don't know how you got a woman."

"I may be a smart-ass, but my ringtone isn't 'The Imperial March,' either. Women—*normal* women—are often put off by that."

"But I've got money. That makes up for a lot, as you well know. Make sure Jamie mentions that to her friends."

"We'll see."

He knew Eric was just being his usual self, but it still left a bad taste in his mouth for some reason. Why *had* Jamie suddenly changed her mind about things between them? If she'd only been lonely—or in need of a human sacrifice—she wouldn't have held back from him for so long. And what did Eric mean by that statement about money making up for a lot? He wasn't rich—yet—but he was pretty comfortable, especially for his age group. If Jamie was looking for a rich guy to take care of her, she probably would have aimed a bit higher than him.

But now that he thought about it, Jamie was still holding back. She still had those walls up, and while he might not have told her everything about his childhood, the last eight years of *her* life were an information black hole.

It was a little strange, but prying into her psyche might make her want to return the favor, and he didn't want to go there. Not yet, at least.

He pushed the thought aside as he parked in front of his house and saw Jamie in the circle of his porch light, frowning at her phone. The frown upended itself as soon as she saw him, and she lifted her free hand to show him the bottle of champagne.

"What are we celebrating?"

"I got the job!"

Then she launched herself into his arms for a kiss, and he forgot what he was so worried about anyway.

CHAPTER EIGHT

COLIN POPPED THE cork on the champagne, and she held out the glasses for him to fill. "I had a message on my phone this afternoon from Kate Roth. I start Monday. It even has benefits, which is awesome."

"Congratulations."

She clinked her glass against his and took a sip, reveling in the taste and the feel of the bubbles on her tongue. It had been so long since she'd had decent champagne, and while it may have been pricey, she'd decided at the store that it was worth the splurge. "Thank you. I'm so excited I'm about to burst."

"I feel like I should take you out somewhere to celebrate."

"That's so sweet. But," she stepped back to model her outfit, "I'm covered in restaurant yuck. I came straight here instead of going home to shower and change first."

"You're welcome to take a shower here. However," Colin stepped closer toward her, "I can't guarantee you'll get to take it alone."

She gave him a half smile. "You say that like it's a bad thing."

She sidled up to him, closing the gap between them, only to have her phone start quacking. She could hear it vibrating against the counter as well. *Ugh. I should have put that on silent.* "Ignore that."

Colin's eyes widened in amusement. "Is your phone *quacking?*"

"Yes."

"Why?" he prodded when she didn't elaborate.

"So I'll know without looking that I don't want to answer it. Wait—"

But Colin had already reached for the phone, helpfully trying to hand it to her, only to be confused by her words. When he looked down at the screen, she cringed inwardly.

An eyebrow went up. "Um, Rotten Bastard is calling."

Suddenly, changing Joey's name in her phone seemed juvenile instead of the empowering swipe of petty revenge she'd felt at the time. "Yeah. Hence the quacking and the ignoring."

"Your ex, I assume."

"Uh-huh."

"I'm now a little worried what comes up when *I* call you."

"Just your name. I promise." Thankfully, the quacking stopped as it went to voice mail.

Colin put the phone down on the counter. "Does he call you a lot?"

Was Colin jealous? Because that sounded a little jealous. "Occasionally. But not a lot. Mainly when he's drunk."

"Why don't you just block him, then?"

"I've thought about it, but there are some…loose ends that still need tying up at some point, and there's always the chance that he's calling about that. If it's important, I'll find out from the voice mail message."

"You made it sound like you made a clean break when you came here, though."

Crap. As if she could explain the four-carat emerald-cut diamond in her safe deposit box that wasn't hers to sell *or* to wear. Or the few pieces of paper she'd signed her name to that the lawyers were still trying to sort out. And until the investigations were complete, she wouldn't be completely rid of him anyway. "We were together a long time. Not everything was able to be a clean or easy break."

Her phone pinged again to tell her she had a voice mail message.

"Do you need to see what he wants?"

"No. It's Friday night. It can't be anything I really want—or need—to hear right now." She made a deliberate show of silencing the ringer and shoving the phone into her purse. She was not going to let Joey rain on her parade tonight.

"You never talk about him."

She tried to keep it light. "I thought that was a good thing. All the dating magazines and websites say not to bore people with rants about your ex."

"There's rants and then there's basic info. If you were with someone for that long, it's normal for things to come up occasionally. In fact, it's a little weird when it doesn't. We all have exes, you know. They're just a part of your life story."

He was like a dog with a bone. What was with him tonight? "But I'm trying to close that chapter."

"You don't have to hide it from me."

"I'm not hiding anything. I don't like bad memories and would rather not wallow in the past." She took a long drink, but the champagne tasted sour now, and she put the glass down, disgusted she'd let this affect her so much and ruin the celebratory mood. Then the words came tumbling out before she could stop them. "Joey's an ass. A lying, cheating ass, and I didn't know it. Even when I had suspicions, I ignored them like a naive idiot. So I'm actually embarrassed I somehow overlooked that very important information during the years I wasted with him. And that's *exactly* why I don't talk about it."

Colin seemed taken aback at her outburst, so she paused to pull herself together. Sour or not, she took another drink just to cool the spurt of anger. "It takes time to fully untangle yourself from some things, even though you might wish it was quicker."

"Do you need a lawyer, Jamie? I can—"

"I don't *need* anything, Colin, except a different topic of conversation."

The silence hung there between them.

Colin finally cleared his throat. "My mom has…problems. Growing up, things could be really good or really bad, and I never really knew what to expect or when things might change and go spiraling into hell. So when you talk about wanting to get your life under control or trying to forget parts of your past, I can relate to that."

Jamie didn't know what to say. This wasn't exactly what she'd expected from a new topic of conversation.

But Colin didn't seem to need her to respond. "She's a little better now, and the medication helps, but it was a long process getting there. I don't like to think about it, much less talk about it, but I can't deny it happened either."

"I'm sorry to hear that." *And it explained some stuff.* "Can I ask why you're telling me this? And why now?"

"So that you know it's okay to tell me stuff. We all come with baggage and backstory. There's no need to be ashamed."

"I appreciate that." She tried to think of something else appropriate to say, because she realized this was a big step for Colin since he'd never mentioned it before. And neither had anyone else who knew him. But her situation was different. She just wasn't sure how to make that distinction without belittling his words. "But your mom's problems weren't really your fault. You have nothing to be ashamed of. The shame comes in when the tragedy of your backstory is that it *is* your fault."

There was another long silence before Colin nodded. "Are you hungry?"

She grabbed onto the change of topic like a life rope. "Actually, I am. How about you order us something and I'll go grab that shower?" It was a rather abrupt, and slightly lame, shift, but she needed the time to gather herself.

She paced as she waited for the water to warm up. Why did Colin have to push? She wasn't some lost soul in need of help, so why did he always try to fix things instead of just minding his own business? She wanted this to be easy, to be something where she could be herself without any pressure. She just needed him to back the hell off.

Part of her figured she should just tell him the whole ugly story. She wasn't running from her past, and she wasn't hiding from it either, but she didn't want it to hold her back. And the only way to do that was to just move on. She couldn't spend the rest of her life looking under the couch cushions for secrets and lies. That much she knew for sure.

What had happened with Joey had nothing to do with who she was or her life now, so there really wasn't a reason to go into it. Except that she would have to tell Colin the full story eventually. Well, only if this was going to get serious.

Frustrated, Jamie got into the shower and gasped as the tepid water hit her skin. *See, this is what happens when you don't think things through and jump in too quickly.*

But you can't not jump, either.

Which meant she needed to quit being embarrassed over the whole thing and come clean with Colin sooner rather than later. He'd shared something important and personal with her, and that seemed like a big step. One that would take them into a new place.

So she needed to tell him. She should tell him.

But not tonight. She needed more prep time before she went there.

Scrubbing the restaurant off her skin gave her time to calm down and clear her head, and by the time she turned off the shower, she felt normal again. At some point, Colin had come in, because a clean T-shirt now sat on top of her towel. It hung nearly to her knees, and between using his soap and wearing his shirt, she almost had the complete Colin smell surrounding her. It made her smile as she combed out her hair.

Barefoot and with her hair still damp, she went back to the kitchen to find Colin unpacking boxes from a white takeout bag. The smell of barbecue filled the air and her stomach audibly growled.

"More champagne?" Colin asked. She loved how he didn't harp on stuff, easily forgetting things that were better left behind. "I don't know how well it will go with ribs, though. There's beer if you prefer."

This was her life now.

And it was pretty damn good. She just wanted to enjoy this part awhile longer.

"Or," he added, "there's soft drinks, since you're driving later."

"I'll finish the champagne and then maybe have a beer." He looked at her oddly, and she took a deep breath. "I mean, I don't have to drive home tonight, right? Maybe I could crash here if I needed to?"

A slow grin spread across Colin's face. "Yeah. You could do that."

Yeah. I could.

For the first time, Jamie was sound asleep in his bed. And not just a catnap before heading back to her place—actual sleep with the intention of waking up there the next morning. It was nice, although he'd quickly discovered she was a bit of a bed hog, taking her half diagonally across the middle.

But that wasn't what was keeping him awake.

Carefully, so as not to disturb her, Colin went to the living room and brought his laptop back up. He sat there for a minute, staring at the Google home page. She must have done the same, he reasoned, to find his address the first time she'd come to his office. It was no big deal.

He typed Jamie's name and hovered over the enter key. It hadn't occurred to him until now to even search for her, since contrary to popular belief, most average citizens didn't have a lot of information readily available or easily accessible out there. Plus, it seemed creepy and stalkerish.

He believed in privacy. He'd had too much of his life examined by neighbors and therapists and doctors not to. He didn't dig into other people's lives because he didn't want them digging into his.

But he hit enter anyway.

There were a lot of Jamie Vincents in the world, both

male and female, and he ended up scrolling through the page of the returned links with only half an eye. Just as he was about to give up, something caught his attention that had him scrolling back to the top: the number of times he saw the name Jamie Vincent in a headline with "Joey." She'd never mentioned her ex's last name, but this had to be a good start.

The first link had a large picture, and he didn't recognize the woman at first. But then he realized that was Jamie, only as a blonde—which partly explained why he'd scrolled right past it before—pictured on the arm of Joey Robbins, who, it turned out, was baseball's latest hottest thing.

That explained her extensive baseball knowledge.

Jamie's ex wasn't just any ex. Colin didn't follow sports, much less baseball, but he did recognize the face from TV commercials for everything from soap to sports drinks.

Well, no wonder Jamie was so freaked out by her new life. She'd gone from pampered fiancée of a pro athlete to waitress in a matter of weeks. This wasn't just starting over; this was having the entire rug jerked out from under her.

Was that why Jamie hadn't blocked him on her phone? Were any of those "loose ends" the hope they'd reconcile? She had to be missing her old life a lot.

Maybe she wasn't as over Joey as she'd claimed. Maybe Colin was just a placeholder until she went back to him and her previous life.

Maybe she considered him a step down from her ex.

None of this sat very well on his mind.

The article beneath the picture wasn't about Jamie, though. Joey, it seemed, was currently suspended from play and under investigation for a string of offenses, including steroid use, betting against his own team and some possibly dodgy tax issues. He was maintaining his innocence, claiming a series of misunderstandings, but this article opined that the evidence was strong against him. His career—and his pricey endorsement deals— were hanging in the balance of the investigation.

Maybe Jamie was waiting to see how it all turned out before she made her final decision.

He started clicking through some of the other links, focusing on Joey instead of just Jamie.

There were also some accusations of other drug use, a DUI and some wild partying with women who weren't Jamie—and might possibly be prostitutes.

Even with such a myriad of evidence and accusations, the consensus seemed to be that he'd survive this with probably only fines and community service. But he wouldn't survive it unscathed; the damage to his reputation was done. Until this exploded, Joey Robbins had been the poster boy of positive sportsmanship, a role model for working hard and doing the right thing. He'd led his college team to take the championship three years in a row, been a standout during his years in the minor leagues, and since he'd been in the majors, his fastball had become a thing of legend and glory.

Additional proof of his all-around goodness was in the eight-year relationship with his college sweetheart, who'd initially stood by him, professing his innocence when the accusations had first hit the papers.

They'd called her naive, foolish and a dumb blonde. Gold digger, silly arm candy.... It was brutal.

No wonder she'd snapped at him when he'd asked her to be his arm candy for the launch party. She was probably good at it, but not proud of the skill.

The news she'd left Joey shortly thereafter was considered pretty conclusive evidence that the accusations were true, and Joey's fans were now vilifying her for turning on him, betraying him, and calling Jamie a liar and a publicity whore.

Jamie couldn't win with those people no matter what she did.

She'd said it was ugly and public. She hadn't been kidding. The question, though, was why she'd kept it so quiet, as though it was *her* dirty secret, not his. If anything, she came out looking pretty good in this.

Except...

She'd been arrested. And hauled in by investigators for questioning. And here was a report of her bank records being subpoenaed. Although this article didn't outright accuse her of anything, it presented more than enough information to make people believe she was hip deep in the same legal and ethical hot water as Joey.

He had a hard time believing *that*.

At the same time, though, what did he really know about her? If you'd asked him an hour ago, he would have said he knew her pretty well, but this information not only called attention to the gaping hole in his knowledge, it also cast a different light on what he *did* know about her.

She claimed embarrassment about what had happened, but no amount of embarrassment really justified the levels of avoidance Jamie attempted. Did she honestly think no one would ever find out?

Didn't people who were wrongly accused protest their innocence loudly? Why wasn't she telling her side of the story to anyone who might listen?

And that made him wonder what else she had to hide.

Hearing footsteps, he quickly closed out the window

and looked up just as Jamie came into the room. She looked tousled and sleepy. "What are you doing up?"

"I couldn't sleep, so I was just browsing around."

She came to sit next to him on the couch and curled up against his arm. "Anything interesting?"

Very. "Just the buzz on this hot new game called *Dungeons of Zhorg.* It's supposedly awesome."

"Sounds fascinating." She sighed and rested her head on his shoulder. "I'd let you tell me all about it, but I'm too tired."

"Then go back to bed. I'll be in in a few minutes."

"Okay." After a quick kiss on the cheek, Jamie looked at him oddly. "Is everything all right?"

"Of course."

He just needed to think for a little while.

A job. A real job where she got to wear nice clothes and not smell like fried stuff at the end of the day. A job where people talked about interesting things—things she'd never even considered before, like how light affected color and mood or how to modernize old buildings without destroying their charm and historical importance.

A full week under her belt and a paycheck in her hand, Jamie didn't know whether to giggle in glee or thank her lucky stars.

So she did both.

Oh, there was a lot to learn, but she was looking forward to it. She was already thinking that maybe next year—after she'd had a chance to really get settled and save up some money—she would look into going back to school. That would delay her getting into her own place, of course, but even though she and Kelsey still hadn't become friends in any real sense, they were getting along fine as roommates.

It wasn't as though she was there a whole lot anyway.

It felt so good to deposit that paycheck that Jamie bought a milkshake to help fight the heat as she did some browsing through the French Market. Talk about savoring… She couldn't remember the last time she'd not been on a diet or living Joey's newest high-protein, low-carb, super-soy-or-something training diets. The milkshake tasted like heaven in a paper cup.

The French Market's stalls of merchandise were hit-or-miss on quality and necessity and highly targeted toward tourists looking to pick up cheap souvenirs, overpriced "art" and low-level knockoffs of designer brands, but it was fun, nonetheless.

She was contemplating a kudzu-blossom-scented candle when something at the next table caught her eye. It was a small clay statue of an old-school computer with a guy in a superhero cape standing on it in a heroic pose. The inscription on the base read, "Alpha Geek."

She laughed out loud.

She'd never heard of the term, but it seemed to fit Colin perfectly. At first glance, he was built more like an athlete—which, as she'd learned when she started spending the night at his place, came from disgustingly early morning runs—but he definitely had an inner geek and a brain full of sci-fi trivia. Ridiculously smart, even in a group of ridiculously smart people, yet not at all unsociable or awkward. He was certainly the alpha dog in his pack of programming wunderkinds.

She had to buy it.

Successfully haggling the price down to twelve dollars—although she would have paid fifteen—gave her another burst of self-satisfaction, and she stopped to buy a pretty gift bag and bow on her way home.

She'd never bought Colin a gift before—not even just

a little cheesy one—and there seemed something rather important and portentous about that step. But they were moving forward, so…

Vaguely wondering how long it would take her to get used to the humidity in this city, she made her way home. When her phone began to ring, she had to juggle her cup, her bags and Colin's gift to get to it, only to realize she didn't recognize the number. Or even the area code.

She was tempted to let it go to voice mail, but she'd given out her cell number to a lot of people this week and couldn't be sure that the call wasn't work related. And while it might be after six on a Friday, she didn't want to be branded a slacker who wasn't willing to go the extra mile when necessary—especially during her first week.

"Hey, sweetheart."

Sneaky little bastard, calling from someone else's phone. "Do not 'sweetheart' me, Joey. In fact, don't talk to me at all."

"Jamie, wait! Don't hang up."

She got the door unlocked and pushed it open with her hip. There was a slim chance this might be important, so she reined in her frustration. But only barely. "What?"

She could almost hear the charm click on, see the lazy smile. "How are you?"

"Does it really matter?"

"It does. I'm worried about you. And I miss you."

She dropped her keys and bags onto the coffee table and sank onto the couch, very glad Kelsey wasn't home. The headache was already starting to throb behind her eyes. "So I've heard."

"Can't we just talk about this?"

"Oh, I think we've talked quite enough. There's nothing you can say that would make any difference."

There was a long, pregnant pause. "I love you."

Ah, hell. "And I believe you when you say that."

"Then why don't you come on home?"

"Because I don't love you anymore." It was harsh, but she'd never said that to him before and he needed to hear it.

"That can't be true." It was a confident, even arrogant, statement, but Jamie knew him way too well not to hear the hurt under it.

She wasn't going to let that stop her from saying what needed to be said, though. "And yet it is. But even if it weren't, your definition of love isn't acceptable to me."

"Those other women meant nothing to me. You have to believe that."

That grated across a nerve that she wasn't aware she had until now. "Yet you were willing to jeopardize your relationship with me in order to sleep with them. You threw away an awful lot to have sex with women who meant nothing to you. That doesn't make it sound any better. In fact, that makes it sound worse."

"I'm so sorry."

"Good," she snapped, unable to help it. "Maybe you'll learn from this experience, grow as a person."

"Jamie, honey, please…"

"I told you when I left that it wasn't just the women. The drugs, the gambling, the lies…I don't even know who you are anymore. Or even if I ever did. But you're certainly not the man I fell in love with." She rubbed a hand over her eyes. "God, I don't know if that's my fault or yours. Maybe this is who you've always been and I just didn't know it. But either way, we're over."

Joey sighed. "I'm going to come down there."

"It's a free country. And New Orleans is a great place, so I'm sure you'll have a blast." She'd said that airily, but let her voice drop so he'd understand that she was serious now. "But if you come near me, I'll have you slapped with a restraining order. Think your image can handle another blow like that right now?"

She heard his sharp intake of breath and had a quiet moment of victory. Joey didn't know what to do with this Jamie. The surge of raw girl power, followed by a punch of I-am-woman-hear-me-roar was the best natural high she'd ever had—outside of sex.

"I gave you eight years, Joey, and for most of them I was really happy. But you're making this worse. Own up to what you've done, be a man and take responsibility. And not just about us. Everything. And then move on and do better. Otherwise…" She sighed. "Please don't make me regret our entire time together."

"So you're really ending it." His voice was flat. "It's over. Just like that."

Finally. Something gets through. "I ended it a long time ago. I'm sorry that you're just now catching up, but I rather thought you would've figured that out when I tried to give you back the engagement ring and moved out."

"That's your ring. I want you to have it. I want you to *wear* it."

"Not going to happen."

"You've met someone down there, haven't you? That's what—"

"Don't go there. You're only embarrassing yourself now." Wow, it truly was amazing what time could do. Three months ago—hell, probably three *weeks* ago—she'd have been pulled into his cajoling and wheedling to listen to his side again, forced to explain herself repeatedly, gotten defensive, and ended up feeling guilty and sad. Instead, she'd said her piece and made her stand. In fact, this conversation had gone on far too long already. "Joey, it's over. Done. Don't call me again."

She hung up before he could say anything else.

Honestly, she felt a little bad. Joey might have hurt her, but she was past the need to hurt him in a retaliatory tit-for-tat game. Then she reminded herself how necessary that conversation had been and pushed the guilt aside.

Because that other feeling in her chest? That was *freedom*.

And while it took a minute for her to process, name and accept it, there was no doubt she was finally free. She didn't have to prove herself to anyone anymore. She didn't have to do anything out of spite or annoyance. Or guilt.

Somehow, after ages of claiming she was going to, that she was *trying* to, the fact that she had, in fact, moved on had slipped up on her without her knowledge.

Wow. Just wow.

She wanted to celebrate. No, actually she wanted to bask in this moment of glory. Colin had a business thing tonight with Eric and the licensing people, but she didn't want to celebrate this with him anyway. This was a personal accomplishment.

She grabbed a bottle of wine and a glass from the kitchen and went to the bathroom, where she filled the tub with hot water and scented oils, and sank into it with a sigh.

Wow.

CHAPTER NINE

SATURDAY NIGHT, JAMIE picked the restaurant and then dragged him to an art show by a group of local artists of questionable talent. When he lodged a protest, she merely shrugged. "I wanted to try something new."

"This is certainly new. And weird."

"Then we'll go. Life's too short to spend it doing weird or boring things." She turned on a dime and headed for the gallery doors. She was nearly outside before it registered for him.

He caught up to her on the sidewalk and steered her toward the car. "Yes, I know. 'You only live once,' and all that."

"Aw, you read my blog post yesterday." She patted his arm before sliding into the passenger seat. "How sweet."

Callie had taken back *The Ex Factor,* but Jamie continued to write one article a week for the blog, freeing up Callie to do other things. She hadn't gained quite the same following as *The Ex Factor,* but she did speak to that twentysomething single woman trying to "find herself." They *loved* her. "Yep. Very inspiring." He closed the door and headed to his side, only to find her staring at him with narrowed eyes.

"Now you're just jerking my chain."

"Maybe a little. It was kind of over the top in its ca

diem, follow-your-dreams-and-your-heart messages, but it's a good point. One well taken."

"I won't apologize for that."

"No one said you needed to."

"I really believe everything I wrote in there," she insisted.

"Then can I ask when you had this epiphany?"

"Interestingly enough, I wrote that before I truly believed it. It's actually a bit prophetic. Maybe I needed to write it and see it before I could live it."

"Oh, good Lord, you're not going all New Age self-help on me, are you?"

"Of course not." She fell silent and looked out the window as he made the short drive back to his place. "But what you think *is* what you believe," she added quietly a couple of minutes later as he unlocked his front door.

"Mmm-hmm, okay. Do you want a drink? Wine? Beer?"

"Wine." She dropped her overnight bag onto the counter and dug through it as he poured. When he turned back around to hand her a glass, there was a small colorful bag centered on the marble island.

"What's this?"

"A present." She had a smile on her face, but she seemed almost shy about it, too.

"What's the occasion?"

"No occasion. Just a gift. Does there need to be a special occasion to give you a present?"

"But I didn't get you anything."

"That's okay. And don't get too excited and build this up before you open it. It's not *that* great of a present." She tilted her head as he reached for the bag. "By the way, when is your birthday?"

"September tenth."

"Mine's January twentieth," she offered. "I'll be twenty-eight."

He knew that already. Several of the articles he'd found online had mentioned her age, and he'd found a photo of Jamie and Joey dated January 20 with a caption that Joey had taken Jamie out for a birthday dinner at a trendy restaurant in Chicago. He wasn't going to tell her that, though. He opened the bag instead and pulled out a small statue. "Alpha geek?"

Jamie grinned from ear to ear. "Yep. Because you are totally the alpha geek. Among your peers, of course, you're definitely the alpha dog, and, for a self-proclaimed geek, you have some strong alpha tendencies."

It was tacky and cheap and perfect. "I love it. Thank you."

"You're very welcome."

He sat it on the counter. "I think I'll take it to work. Let everyone know who's the boss."

"Okay, but be careful with it. The lady at the French Market says it's one of a kind."

"Yeah, well, the alpha geek is a rare breed."

She nodded solemnly. "Very true. I can't imagine there's a huge population of y'all out there." She winked at him. "I can't say that I mind, though. I like the fact you're unique. I've never met anyone quite like you before."

"I find that hard to believe. That stereotype isn't as accurate as you might think."

"I never ran with the smart kids, so I wouldn't know. In high school I pretty much stayed within a small social circle."

"Let me guess. Cheerleaders?"

"Dance team. The cheerleaders were easy," she said primly, sipping at her wine. "Then I went to Caroli

State and joined *their* dance team, and that caused me to hang out with more athletes. I didn't exactly branch out. Then I met Joey, and all his friends became my friends."

It was the first time Jamie had ever talked about that part of her life. "I didn't know you went to Carolina State. What was your major?"

"Economics, believe it or not."

"No wonder you had such a hard time finding a job," he teased.

"I had a hard time finding a job because I didn't graduate. I left after my sophomore year. Never even took an upper level econ class, so I don't actually know all that much about economics. Pretty sad, huh?"

That would have been when Joey went into the minor leagues and moved to Texas to play. Jamie had obviously gone with him. "It happens more often than you might think. People leave school for all kinds of reasons."

"Well, I left with Joey. I was sure I'd enroll at another school and finish, but we moved around so much that it was just a nightmare. Credits wouldn't transfer, program requirements would change between the different schools…. It was a mess. And we were struggling moneywise, so that didn't help, especially once it got to the point where my transcripts were so full of incompletes and credit hours that didn't apply to graduation that I lost financial aid eligibility." She shrugged.

He topped off her glass and leaned on his elbows against the bar. "But surely once Joey moved to the major league, things got stable enough so that you could've ︙k."

︙, but by then, it hardly seemed worth it Or nec-
︙Jamie sighed and drank deeply from her glass.
︙he froze, eyes narrowing. A second later, she

turned that narrowed gaze on him. "How do you know Joey played major league ball?"

Ah, damn. "It wasn't that hard to put together," he hedged. "Jamie, Joey, your encyclopedic baseball knowledge…"

"But you don't follow sports. You have no reason to be able to put that together."

He picked up his glass and drank deeply instead of answering.

Crossing her arms over her chest, Jamie raised an eyebrow at him. "Name me one other major league pitcher."

He couldn't. He didn't even try.

"Oh. My. God. You looked me up on the internet?"

He couldn't deny it at this point. "Yes, of course. Everyone does it."

"Stalkers, maybe. Normal people don't."

"If you hadn't been all lady-of-mystery about your ex and why you moved here, I wouldn't have had to."

"And it never occurred to you that I might want to protect my privacy? That there was a *reason* I didn't offer up my life story to people?"

"Privacy? For God's sake, Jamie, you have your own Twitter hashtag."

She flushed. It seemed she didn't like being reminded of that. "Which is exactly why I don't go announcing who I am to everyone I meet." Jamie rubbed her temples. "You looked me up. I can't believe you did that." She was talking more to herself than him, so he stayed quiet. Her head came up slowly. "When?"

"When what?"

"When did you do it?"

He might be able to save himself once she realize he hadn't done it until after they were already involv

"Just a week or so ago. That night you stayed over for the first time."

"Was that what you were doing on the internet in the middle of the night? Running a background check on me? While I was sleeping in your *bed?*"

Okay, so maybe not. "I was curious. Can you blame me? We were getting more…involved and you had this big secret. I felt I needed to know who I was getting involved with."

"You could have *asked* me."

"Would you have actually answered?"

"We'll never know, will we, because you decided to search the internet for dirt instead."

"Not for dirt—"

"But that's what you got. Because I know exactly what's out there, and you'll notice that no one ever asked me for *my* side of the story. You got the salacious tabloid version of my life." She paused. "Wait…did you believe it? I mean, you certainly didn't ask me about it."

"It looks like you got mixed up in something. I'm not saying it was your fault—"

"I didn't get mixed up in squat. The *only* thing I'm guilty of in that mess is naïveté. Everything else is fall-out. I got arrested because I was with a group of people who were doing wrong, but *I* was ignorant of that until the cops showed up. Those charges were dropped, by the way, not that *that* information made the blogs," she grumbled. "My life was ripped apart and examined under a microscope because no one was willing to believe that I was stupid enough not to know what was going on around me. I don't know which is worse—the fact that I was falsely accused or that I really *was* too stupid to know."

"Well—"

She cut him off. She was pacing and probably didn't

even realize he'd tried to say anything. "I defended Joey because I believed in him. And I believed in him because I loved him. That just makes me look like a fool. So no, it's not a part of my life I'm super proud of at the moment, and therefore I don't randomly drop it into idle conversation. I'm not a woman of mystery. I'm just a girl who got screwed and didn't want to brag about her shame." Her cheeks were red and a vein throbbed in her neck.

"I think you're overreacting."

"And I don't think you get to tell me how I should or should not feel about anything," she snapped.

"Well, how was I supposed to feel? When we first met, you disappeared without a trace. The second time we met, you completely blew me off. Then all of a sudden, you're all over me. What brought about *that* change?"

"I got to know you better? Decided you were someone I wanted to spend time with?"

"Only after you found out who I was."

She paused in her pacing. "What's that supposed to mean?"

"You only changed your tune when you found out I wasn't just a bartender at the Lucky Gator."

"Oh, so I'm some kind of gold digger to boot. Lovely." She snorted. "Don't flatter yourself, honey. You've got a nice place here and a good business and all, but it's the lifestyle I'd grown accustomed to."

That was true. But it still stung. As though s she was slumming or something. "Yeah, but it be lifestyle you're currently living."

"Joey still wants me back, and if money was al after, I'd be with him."

"Well, it sounds to me like you're not really ov anyway, so maybe you should go back to him."

"*What?* Jeez, in the movies, when the heroin

up the good life and takes on the struggle on principle, it's all inspirational and stuff. But if you do it in real life, you get nothing but crap and derision."

"That's where you're wrong. I respected what you were trying to do. It takes guts and hard work. I even told Kate that, and that was before I looked you up."

"Kate, as in Kate Roth, my new boss?" Her voice was flat but deadly. "You talked to her about me?"

It was a good thing he only had two feet. At least he didn't have another one to shove into his mouth. "I've known Kate since high school. So yeah, I did. Only good things, though. It's not like I ratted you out or anything. I emailed her before I even knew who you were. Hell, Kate would have researched you as soon as she had your résumé. She probably knew more about you than I did at the time. I just put in a good word, that's all."

That didn't help. If anything, Jamie's lips pressed tighter together with each word he spoke. She finally managed to pry them apart, and her tone would have cut glass. "A good word. Exactly *when* did you put in this good word with Kate?"

There was no sense hedging this time. "I emailed her when you told me you had the second interview. I figured it might help put you in the lead for the job."

"I can*not* believe you."

"What? It worked, didn't it? You got the job you wanted. Why are you so mad?"

"Because I wanted to get the job by myself. Not as a favor to someone. I wanted to be hired on my own merits."

"I'm sure you were."

"But once again, we'll never know, will we?" She started to say something else, then threw her hands up in disgust. "My God, why am I even still here having this conversation? This is insane." She grabbed her wrap, found her shoes and picked up her bag.

"You're leaving?"

"Definitely. I don't know who the hell you are. Or even who you *think* you are, but I'm out of here."

She was completely overreacting. "I was trying to help."

"You really can't see the problem, can you?"

"Honestly, no."

"This is *my* life. *I* make the rules. You don't get to play God or meddle in things that aren't your business. You told me once that if I wanted supreme ultimate power and control, I had to design my own game. Well, you know what? I have. And you don't get to play anymore. Game over."

And with that, Jamie walked out, slamming the door behind her.

Fury drove her out into the street only for her to realize she didn't have a car here at Colin's, and she now had a long walk home.

Good. She needed to walk it off. It wasn't that late, the streets were lit and there were still plenty of other folks out to make her trek perfectly safe. She did pause long enough to pull a pair of flip-flops out of her bag and change her shoes. She wasn't going to risk breaking a heel off her favorite pair of Jimmy Choos on New Orleans' questionable sidewalks just because Colin Raine was a giant ass.

How *dare* he? It was bad enough that he'd dug up dirt on her, but he should have had the guts to come to her with what he'd found. Not that she owed anyone explanations or anything, but it took a real jerk to go lookin for info he knew she wasn't willing to share and then p tend that he didn't know. And to contact her boss? Oh, that just steamed her. A normal person would have said he knew Kate and asked if she *wanted* a plug or not first.

Especially since he claimed he understood—and respected—what she was trying to do. *Argh.*

What was it about her that made people think she was an idiot? Someone who couldn't manage her own life without assistance? Her parents had offered to help her, but she hadn't wanted the admission of failure or the strings that would have been attached. She'd lost everything and everyone had expected her to fail, but she'd managed to land on her feet—however unsteadily at first.

She'd done pretty damn well, if she did say so herself. And she was proud of it.

The job had been quite a feather in her cap, but even that was tainted a bit now. She should resign on principle, but damn it, she *liked* that job. There was nothing to gain from quitting out of spite. It'd be like shooting herself in the foot. She'd just have to prove to Kate she was more than capable of handling the job and that Kate had made the right decision in hiring her.

She was covering ground quickly, letting anger and autopilot move her feet. What she didn't like, though, was the hurt that was starting to creep in as the anger burned off.

Damn it, she shouldn't be hurt. She should be angry. She *needed* to be angry, because she was damn tired of being hurt. Hurt was what had driven her to move cross-country. Well, that and shame, but she had nothing to be ashamed of this time.

And while part of her wanted to pack up and move someplace else to try again, she wasn't going to give in ‑ that. She liked New Orleans. She could see herself ‑ng very happy here—eventually.

Maybe this was good. Maybe Colin was just meant to be her rebound guy, someone to hold onto while she was figuring things out. She'd just confused rebound feelings for real feelings.

But she was done rebounding. She was also done with shame and hiding from her past.

Unfortunately Kelsey was home, so Jamie had to claim illness to avoid conversation and escape to her room.

Her eyes were burning, and she fought against it. She hadn't cried since that first night she'd found out that Joey had been cheating on her and lying to her. After that one time, she'd refused to cry again.

Until now.

CHAPTER TEN

NO MATTER HOW Colin measured it, the launch party was a success. *Zhorg*'s landscapes were projected against the walls of the room, and a dragon with an eight-foot wingspan hovered overhead. Models—both male and female—hired from a local agency roamed the room in costume, posing for pictures. Caitlyn Reese-Marshall, the actress who'd voiced one of the characters, signed autographs and charmed the press, while the developers demonstrated highlights from the game at stations around the room.

The food was fantastic, everyone seemed to be having a good time *and* being duly impressed by *Zhorg*'s graphics and interface, and they were definitely going to get good press from the event.

And Jamie had been right: he'd gotten many compliments on his suit.

Only she wasn't here to gloat about that.

He'd finally accepted the fact that Jamie wasn't coming. Part of him had held onto the hope that she'd calm down overnight and show up anyway, but after two hours of watching the door with one eye while shaking hands and schmoozing with people, he'd realized that wasn't ~~go~~ing to happen. He had to assume that she'd had the last ~~wor~~d when she walked out last night.

Not that he understood *why* she was so mad. And not that he should be all that surprised that she'd overreacted so spectacularly—he'd conveniently forgotten the way she could swing to extremes—and that she had no problem just disappearing whenever it suited her.

But that still didn't keep him from wanting her here—if for no other reason than it showcased how successful he and Rainstorm Games were. It might not be on the same level as a pro ball player's party, but it wasn't exactly the minor leagues, either.

For God's sake, why on earth was he mooning over Jamie not being here? This was a big night—for him, for Eric and for Rainstorm—and even if he wasn't enjoying it, he damn well needed to be working it.

He'd told Callie weeks ago when she started this whole business with Jamie that he didn't have time for it, that his Cinderella would just have to be a footnote in this biography one day. Had she listened? No, of course not. The woman who constantly wanted him to butt out of *her* life had shamelessly butted herself right into his. He had the urge to go unleash something nasty into her computer's hard drive.

It wouldn't change anything, but it *would* make him feel better.

And at least that was something.

Jamie kept one eye on the TV as she loaded clothes into bags. She was sorry to see some of them go—especially that adorable Hugo Boss tweed skirt—but her new lack of a diet and the fabulous New Orleans food had added several pounds to her frame, and she couldn't get it zipped anymore. That skirt was almost cute enough to make her reconsider and go back on a diet, but the truth was she liked her new curves. She also liked not worrying abo her weight or going to Pilates classes four days a week, so sacrifices had to be made.

Plus, the manager at the women's shelter had told her that they could sell the clothes through a consignment shop and use the money instead. Jamie was fine with that. She hadn't paid for any of her wardrobe, so she didn't feel comfortable consigning them herself. She didn't need the money that badly, and the shelter could do good things with the cash.

And no one needed that many clothes anyway. She wasn't in any danger of having to go naked any time soon.

Plus, her wardrobe needs were pretty basic at the moment. She worked; she came home. In a way, she'd backslid in her progress, and while she loved her job, she was just as lonely as she'd been when she first arrived in town. It wasn't that she didn't know people—her circle of acquaintances grew each day—but the one person she wanted to spend time with was off-limits.

God, she missed him.

But she was staying strong and not giving in to the urge to call him. Time might have given her perspective on what had happened, but she couldn't get past the fact Colin had lied to her and gone behind her back—for whatever reason.

He didn't trust her. And she couldn't trust him.

So it was for the best. She knew all too well how painful important lessons were to learn, but she was learning. And it wasn't as though she hadn't been in this position before.

Jeez, how many times would she have to hit the reset button on her life before she got it right?

Finally, the TV station cut away from the talking heads a table with a single microphone. Jamie grabbed the

remote and turned up the volume. Joey's press conference would be starting any second.

All in all, Joey was going to get off lightly. According
to yesterday's newspaper, investigators hadn't been able
to find enough proof to continue pursuing the possibility of illegal activity. They'd all but said they believed
him to be guilty of much more only they couldn't find
evidence to support it.

*Because while Joey can be an idiot, he's not that stu-
pid.*

They had him on the smaller things, even though those
were more immoral than illegal.

So a fine, a short suspension...yeah, Joey was one
lucky guy. She had no idea how many of his endorsement
deals had dropped him or how much his career might
suffer in the future, but he was going to walk away from
this with far less than he deserved.

Joey had done a lot of damage and now she wanted
to see him apologize. And that was the only reason she
was going to watch his press conference.

When Joey took the microphone, she was surprised to
see how tired he looked. No one else would notice, but
she knew him too well. He also had a bandage wrapped
around his thumb, another sure sign of the stress he'd
been feeling, but also another detail no one else would
notice, because she was probably the only person who
knew Joey would chew his thumbnail until it bled when
he was upset over something. But to the average, casual
observer, he looked fit, healthy and confident.

After the expected denials, weasel words and evasions,
he looked straight at the camera. "And to everyone I've
hurt—my friends, my fans, my teammates and my loved
ones—I'm sorry. Please believe that and believe me when

I say I'm going to work to be a better person from now on. I hope you'll give me the chance to prove that to you."

Oddly, she didn't get any satisfaction from seeing him humbled like that. She'd watched so she could close the door on all of it, but when she didn't feel any different, she realized she already had.

Turning off the TV, she grabbed her bags and drove to the women's shelter, singing along to a CD instead of listening to the rehash of the press conference on the radio.

The manager of the shelter met her in the lobby to help off-load the bags. "This is very kind of you."

"It's my pleasure. I'm going to need a receipt, please."

As another woman went to get the receipt, Jamie saw the manager reach down and pull out the blue bag sitting on top and remove the small box inside. There might as well have been a sign on top of it that said Very Expensive Jewelry. "Did you mean for this to be in here?"

"Yes. He doesn't want it back and I can't keep it. Like the clothes, I'd feel uncomfortable selling it and keeping the money myself. I'd rather you did something worthwhile with what you can get for it."

"Do you mind if I take a look?"

"Of course not."

Jamie heard her gasp as she opened the top. She'd made a similar noise when Joey had handed her that box years ago. It was a gaspworthy ring, but it was too ostentatious for her taste and she'd always felt awkward wearing it. "Oh, *my*. Are you sure?"

"Very sure. All the paperwork on the diamonds is in the bag, so you should be able to sell it to a reputable jeweler without any problems." The other woman arrived with the receipt and gasped as well when she saw the ring. Jamie quickly filled it out and stuck it in an envelope with Joey's name and address on the outside. "Thank you and have a great day."

"Ms. Vincent, can I—just so that I know when I take it in and can negotiate properly with the jeweler—can I ask if you know the approximate value of the ring?"

Jamie stopped with one hand on the door. She had to think for a minute. To her, it was worthless. "About sixty, sixty-five thousand."

At the woman's wide-eyed gawk, Jamie bit back a smile. This was the most pleasure she'd gotten from that ring in a long time.

Outside the shelter's office, she dropped the envelope with the donation receipt for Joey into the mailbox. He could choose to write it off on his taxes or not.

She was one hundred percent done with all of it.

Life started now.

Life after the launch was busy for Colin and Rainstorm. There was the public stuff—follow-up requests from the media, gaming forums to keep an eye on, advertising campaigns to tweak—and then there was the inside stuff, like hackers to thwart, bots to squash, servers to monitor, bugs to fix.

Once upon a time, he'd thrived on this. Twelve-and sixteen-hour days used to slide by quickly, making things like sleep and food unnecessary. He wished he had that kind of focus and ability to get lost in the work now.

Colin had forgotten what not having a life was like. Funny how lack of a life hadn't bothered him until he'd tasted how the other half lived, and now he found his existence less than gratifying. Sadly, he didn't have a reason anymore to escape. His place would be just as disappointing, only with the added depressive knowledge of what it used to be like.

And to top it all off, *Eric* had a date tonight, a fact he'd all but crowed about until Colin had been ready to punch him.

So when his phone rang and Callie's number popped up on the screen, he answered it happily, grateful for the distraction. "What's up?"

"Did you fall and hit your head recently?"

Okay. "What? No. Why?"

"Because you're acting pretty damn dumb for a genius and that's the only explanation I can come up with."

Now he remembered why he shouldn't have answered the phone. Callie wasn't just a distraction, she was a frustration. And he wasn't in the mood for it. "I don't know what you're talking about."

"I'm on the sidewalk outside your office. Come let me in and I'll explain it in small words and simple sentences."

Good thing Elise had locked the door when she'd left for the evening about an hour ago, or else Callie would have been able to barge right in. "I'm working."

"Colin Eliot Raine…"

"Fine." He sighed and went through the lobby to flip the lock on the double glass doors. "Lovely to see you, Callie, so glad you could drop by," he said with sarcastic cheerfulness.

"How did you manage to screw up so royally with Jamie?"

At least Callie wasn't one to beat around the bush. He found that trait to be rather annoying. "It didn't work out. These things happen."

"Really? It just *happened.* You didn't act like a royal ass or anything." Sarcasm dripped off each word.

"Jamie is the one who overreacted to basically *everything* and walked out on me."

"I don't blame her."

Great. "So Jamie came to you to spill her guts."

Callie dropped dramatically onto one of the sofas in the reception area. "She didn't have to. I read the blog post she wrote for tomorrow."

"*What?* Jamie wrote a blog post about me?"

"Not by name, no. But since I know you, I can read between the lines. It's not that hard to figure out. So what did you do?"

"Beats the hell out of me."

Callie sighed and rolled her eyes. "Try again."

He shrugged. Without knowing what Jamie had written, he went with the easiest explanation. "I looked her up on the internet. It's a common thing."

"Oh, I can only imagine how well that went over when she found out."

Maybe Callie could provide insight into the female mind and explain why the hell Jamie was so bent out of shape. "To listen to her, though, you'd think I hacked into her computer and read her diary instead of gathering what is essentially public information."

"Let me guess—you didn't tell her you knew all this info about her. I looked her up, too—probably before you did, so I know what you found. I can only imagine how embarrassed she was."

He shook his head. "She wasn't embarrassed. She was pissed."

"Trust me, it's all in the same category." She motioned for him to come sit next to her. "How would you like it if I'd told Jamie embarrassing stories about you from high school?"

That stopped him short. "*Did* you?" He might have to kill her.

"No, but that's not the point. When you did find out,

you'd wonder if she'd been secretly laughing at you behind your back or judging you based upon that information. I'll forgive you the search. But you should have told her. Asked her about it, at least."

"I apologized."

Callie snorted. "Hopefully not in the same defensive way you just acted when I brought it up."

Damn it, she had a point.

"My question, though, is what *else* did you do?"

He shrugged again. "I sent an email to Kate Roth when Jamie was interviewing with her."

She rubbed her hands over her face. "Jesus, Colin, will you never learn?"

"I was trying to help. Why is that a bad thing?"

She leveled a look at him. "Did she *ask* you to?"

"No." Because Jamie wasn't Callie, who had an old bone to pick.

Callie rolled her eyes and sighed. "Then why did you do it?"

"I knew she wanted the job, and I wanted to put in a good word for her."

"So why is she mad at you?"

Finally. He felt vindicated. "That's exactly *my* point. She's overreacting."

Patting his arm, she shook her head. "Um, let me rephrase, because I wasn't agreeing with you. My question for you is *why* did that make her angry?"

"She says she wanted to get the job herself. Without help."

"I can't really fault her on that. Especially knowing what she's been through, I can see why that would be important to her."

"But I didn't *know* about her ex and all that trauma when I did it."

"That doesn't matter, honey. My point is, you should have asked her first if she wanted your help."

He couldn't really rebut that, considering the current situation he was in. "I meant well. Doesn't that count for something?"

"Of course. But here's a news flash for you, Colin. You don't always know what's best for people. They don't always need you to swoop in and save the day. It's sweet and all, but it's also *really* annoying. And sometimes it makes things worse. You have to learn to let people ask for help. Or at least offer first and give them the opportunity to decline the assistance."

"So I'm supposed to stand there and watch them fall on their asses."

"Sometimes that's what you have to do. I know it's hard, but that's how some people learn. Sometimes they want—or need—that experience. I know I did."

"You failed pretty spectacularly."

Callie's mouth twisted. "Yes, and thank you for the reminder. But the thing is, life is messy and chaotic. People screw up and make mistakes and you can't always stop them. And you can't always save them either. But everyone who knows you knows that they can count on you. And that's awesome."

Mollified and feeling less like the bad guy, he patted her leg. "Thank you."

She smacked him in return. "But that doesn't make it less annoying when you cross that line. And it certainly doesn't put you in the right when you do it, either. Jamie has every reason to be pissed at you."

He should have known that was too good to last. "Well, she did the same thing you did when I crossed that line. She dumped me."

"Yeah, but you refused to apologize to me. That didn't help."

"I've already apologized to her. It didn't help."

"Then apologize again. Sincerely. Explain—without getting huffy—why you did it and ask her to forgive you. I have a feeling she wants to."

He looked at her sideways and snorted. "And exactly how do you know that?"

"Because I read her blog entry. Maybe you should, too." After another of those slightly condescending pats, she stood and put her bag over her shoulder. "I came here as a friend, because I think Jamie makes you happy, and I really want you to be happy. But this is on you to fix. Maybe *fix* is the wrong word," she corrected. "This is *on* you because you were in the wrong. Take responsibility for that. You can't change what happened, but you can apologize, and promise to do better from now on. So do that." With that, Callie smiled encouragingly and let herself out.

He locked the door behind her and went back to his office. There were still bots and scripts and hackers needing his attention, but he ignored them for the moment. He had a lot to think about.

It was interesting that Callie hadn't asked him the same question he hadn't asked himself: Did he want Jamie back in his life?

Callie obviously assumed the answer was yes, otherwise she wouldn't have offered him advice on how to go about it.

He was miserable, but he'd blamed lack of sex and too much work—mainly because he didn't want to think about Jamie. Because the truth was, he missed her terribly.

He respected the way Jamie had taken control of her

life, walking away from what she knew and starting over from scratch. And while it had made her a little crazy, she'd had good reason to be. She'd faced the fear and the uncertainty and gotten through it without ever losing faith in herself.

Her wholehearted embrace of her new life was inspiring and her enthusiasm for it was contagious.

Callie was right. Life was messy and chaotic, but that was just a fact he had to deal with. Not all chaos and mess were necessarily bad anyway. They made things interesting.

He'd lived in his own bubble, head down and nose to the grindstone, for so long he'd forgotten what it was like to not be like that, and it explained his dissatisfaction simply. It wasn't the lack of a life he was missing; it was the lack of Jamie in his life.

He liked Jamie's chaos. And her special brand of crazy.

Actually, he loved it. And he loved her.

And that brought the realization that it wasn't her baggage that was the problem. It was his.

Could I have screwed this up worse?

Jamie's blog post wasn't up on the site, but it was easy enough to find in the scheduled queue for tomorrow.

My name is Jamie Vincent. That won't mean anything to many of you, and I'm glad of that. For those of you thinking "that Jamie Vincent?" the answer is yes, that Jamie Vincent. And for those of you who just went and looked me up, now you know why I was glad you didn't know who I was. I don't have anything to add to what's already out there, other than to, once again, insist that I had no knowledge of what was going on. You don't have to believe that, but I'm not going to revisit that subject ever again. It's over. It's done. I've moved on.

I always felt a bit dishonest whenever I gave advice on people's lives on this site—much less about their love lives—because, deep down, I felt like I was in no position to offer good advice after the mess I'd made of my own life. But I look back over those posts now and I think I did pretty well. Maybe because I was talking to myself in some way, saying the things I really needed to hear.

The one thing I've learned from all of this is to trust myself. There's very little in life that can't be fixed if you're willing to really try. And you have to be willing to not only trust yourself, but others, too.

Never be ashamed of what's driving you, but don't be driven by shame. It's true that what doesn't kill you will only make you stronger, but you might just have been stronger than you thought all along. And while it's near impossible to truly forget, much less forgive, all the wrongs that were done to you, holding onto those wrongs gives them the power to hold you back and hold you down.

If you're trapped by your past, you miss the present and the future.

Life's too short for that.

Well, one thing was clear: Jamie wasn't hung up on her ex. And she certainly didn't have plans to go back to him now that the investigation was over, as she was still in town and every celebrity gossip website had pictures of him out with another woman.

He could see Callie's point. He wasn't going to pretend Jamie had written that solely for his benefit, but if this was an honest piece, there might be a way for him to apologize and explain.

Because while they weren't supposed to be anything at all, somewhere along the line they had become something. To him, at least.

He wanted that back.

Because he wanted to see where else it would go.

And now he just had to convince Jamie of that.

Jamie limped along Bourbon Street, blood streaming out of a leg wound. She needed to find a doctor—and soon—but first...

The zombie hit her from behind, sending her to her knees. She tried to roll, but it had her by the legs... The picture on the screen froze, turning red, then black. She was dead.

Again.

She pulled off her headphones in frustration, tossing them onto the table beside her laptop. "Ah, damn it."

"It's a tricky level." Colin's voice came from behind her, causing her to jump. He stood in the doorway between the living room and the dining room, hands in his pockets, looking uncomfortable. "Kelsey let me in," he said by way of explanation.

She had no idea what to say. The little spark of happiness that had flared in her chest at seeing him here was damped by the questions of what and why and all the embarrassment and...this was more than a little awkward. It would have been awkward to see him for the first time after she stormed out no matter what the circumstances were, but having him catch her playing his game—and sucking at it—just added to that feeling. "How long have you been standing there?"

He smiled slightly. "Long enough to see the mistake that made you zombie snacks."

At least she could cover some of the awkwardness. The game gave her a safe topic of conversation while she searched for her composure. "So you could tell me what I did wrong?"

"I could." He paused for a moment, and then said, "Or I could wait and let you figure it out on your own. I know how that can make things much more satisfying."

One of the knots in her stomach loosened. But it figured that he'd work that nugget of wisdom out only when she was completely stymied by his oddly addictive and utterly frustrating game. "This is the fourth time I've died on this exact spot. I don't think I'm going to ever figure it out."

An eyebrow went up. "Fourth? That's not good."

"Why?" She looked back at the screen, where her character had regenerated five blocks from Bourbon Street. She'd lost more experience points, of course, but everything else seemed— "No! It took my flamethrower!"

"And your spare shotgun shells, if you had any." The corner of his mouth twitched. "And I guess I should warn you, that if it catches you a fifth time in that same spot, you'll get bitten and start to zombiefy yourself."

"Oh, for God's sake. This is impossible. How the hell am I supposed to get past it?"

"Are you asking for help?"

This conversation would actually be funny if it weren't so serious and layered with all kinds of personal hang-ups. "Yes."

Colin pulled a chair over to sit next to her and reached for the keyboard. At the last second, he pulled his hand back. "Do you want me to tell you what to do or just give you a hint?"

Another knot in her stomach untied. That was kind of sweet. Maybe he really had learned something. "How about you give me a hint."

Colin thought for a second. "Choose stealth over aggression."

Based on everything that had happened in this level to this point, that seemed counterintuitive and a good way to die again. "Are you sure?"

He laughed. "Um, yeah. I designed the game, remember?"

He did have a point there. But since they weren't—or at least she wasn't—talking strictly about the game… "I'm not sure I like the idea of stealth. I prefer facing things head on."

"I like that about you. And I've come to appreciate it myself. However, at the time I put this game together, my views were a little different. I've changed—some might even say grown—since then."

"I see."

Colin took a deep breath. "I was a jerk. And I'm sorry. I should have asked you before contacting Kate. While I had only the best of intentions, that doesn't make it right. I have a tendency to step in before I'm asked to do so. It's a habit. My mom was—is—bi-polar and was unmedicated for years. When I said things could get chaotic and bad, I meant it. I didn't like the uncertainty or the constant picking up of the pieces. Callie says I now tend to try to get control too quickly and start to sort things out before I'm asked for my help."

She hadn't been ready for that big of a revelation. *That explained a lot.* Not only his annoying habit of trying to fix everything, but also his need to control things in his life. She was only surprised he hadn't been worse about it. "I know you meant well. But I'm not in need of help. Or fixing. Regardless of how big a mess my life might be."

He shrugged. "I realize that now. And I can only promise not to butt in unless I'm asked to in the future. It's a hard habit to break, but I'm going to try."

She nodded.

Colin cleared his throat. "And while I'm apologizing… I should have respected your privacy and not looked you up online. But once I did, I should have told you."

That was embarrassing, but not only for the reasons he thought. He'd been honest with her, though, so she owed him some in return. "I'm starting to realize that I was a bit oversensitive about Joey and what happened. I was trying to forget it all—and afraid people might judge me for it—and I went a little too far. I can't actually blame you for looking me up, considering how evasive I was about it. In your shoes, I probably would have done the same thing."

"But still…" *Boy, he really was in apology mode.* "I should have trusted you and respected you enough to be honest. Not only about—" He stopped. "Actually, I should have been honest about everything."

The knots that had been loosening tightened up again. She didn't want there to be an everything. The building hope in her chest didn't have a place for an everything that might screw this up. She didn't want proof that she'd been wrong about Colin, that he had secrets—bad secrets—that she'd been unaware of and that he now felt the need to confess. She didn't want to believe that she'd been blind or played for a fool again.

Every nerve ending in her body was reaching out for him, and only sheer force of will was keeping her hands in her lap. Obviously, part of her didn't care what he'd done or not done, and it was more than willing to forget about everything that had happened if he would just touch her, hold her.

She swallowed hard and cleared her throat. She had to know. "Everything?"

"Well, one thing, mainly."

"And that would be…?"

"I wasn't completely honest with you—or myself, actually. I think when I found out your ex was a famous athlete, I became unsure of myself. Like there was no way a geek could ever compete with a jock and win the girl."

Jamie had to bite her lip to keep from saying anything.

"And then when you found out what I'd done, I should have apologized and told you that I'd done it because I was falling in love with you. It wouldn't have made it right—or even less wrong—but it would have been the truth, and you deserved that."

Jamie had gotten stuck at the falling-in-love part. Colin had never seemed to be that invested, and the news shocked her at the same time as it sent a glow through her veins like a healing balm. Her chest was tight, making it hard to breathe, much less get enough air to respond. Even if she could figure out what to say.

Then he smiled crookedly. "I tried stealth, but that didn't work. And aggression doesn't seem like the right thing either. So I'm going to have to go with straightforward and simple."

Jamie realized she was holding her breath now. Then Colin reached for her hand and caressed her fingers as he spoke.

"I'm sorry. And I can't undo what I did, but I can promise to be honest with you from now on, no matter what. And I'm in love with you, so I'm hoping you'll accept this as truth and give me another chance."

* * *

Well, that speech might win the prize for cheesiest thing ever said, but he'd said it, and he meant it. And Jamie certainly looked shocked. In fact, she looked a little pale, and he didn't think she was breathing, either.

That wasn't the reaction he'd been hoping for, that was for sure. He'd been hit by hope when he'd seen her sitting there, wearing that Lucky Gator shirt she'd gotten at Mardi Gras and playing his game, easily convincing himself that those were signs she missed him.

And that he might have a chance to fix this—properly, of course.

Jamie finally seemed to snap out of it, taking a deep breath and squaring her shoulders. "I wasn't completely honest with you, either. I should have been more upfront about who I was and what I was dealing with, but I couldn't bring myself to do it. But it wasn't all just about the embarrassment. Some of that was residual Joey stuff being taken out on you, which really wasn't fair."

She swallowed hard again. "And I was scared. That's really hard for me to admit, because I've tried so hard not to be. But if I hadn't been scared, I'd have been able to be honest with you and realized sooner that I was in love with you."

He had to be hallucinating. While he'd secretly harbored all kinds of ideal outcomes, his *best* case scenario was that she might give him another shot. But now that this had ended up better than expected…

"Colin?"

The sound of his name snapped him out of his thoughts, but the amused tone of her voice caught him off guard. "Yeah?"

She was smiling. "This would be a really good time to kiss me."

So not a hallucination, after all. "With pleasure."

Jamie met him more than halfway, climbing into his lap and straddling him as she melted into him. There was passion and promise in her kiss and a whole wealth of things he couldn't wait to explore.

She broke the kiss long enough to whisper, "My room is right down the hall, second door on the right."

Colin didn't need to be told twice. "Thank God. I've been vibrating on the edge since the moment I walked in." He pushed to his feet without dislodging her, and she clung to his neck as he walked. "And let me tell you," he teased, "seeing you take on the zombies was very sexy."

"I was missing you. It sounds strange, but the game helped. Some," she amended, "even if I do suck at it."

In her tiny room, he kicked the door shut behind him and eased down onto the bed. His whole body seemed to sigh in relief. "You're not bad for a newb. And I'd be happy to teach you all the tricks and strategies and…"

Jamie cupped his cheek in her hand, a small smile playing across her lips. "Can I ask you something?"

"Of course," he replied against her neck as his fingers skimmed under her T-shirt.

"It won't make a difference—with us, I mean—if you say no."

He pushed up onto his elbows to see her face. He wasn't too proud to admit that he was a little worried now. "What is it, Jamie?"

"It's about your game."

"What about it?"

"You said it's your world, right? Ultimate complete control and all that."

Where on earth was she going with this? "Yeah. And?"

"Then can you get me my flamethrower back?"

He was laughing as he kissed her.

EPILOGUE

CALLIE PLANNED THEIR wedding.

A wise man would have seen what was coming and nipped it in the bud, but Callie and Jamie had—rather disturbingly, when he thought too much about it—become good friends recently, and by the time he figured out their plan, it was too late.

And now it was Mardi Gras in October, complete with a second line and a ride through the Quarter from Woldenberg Park to the reception hall on Esplanade in heavily decorated convertibles so the wedding party could throw beads to the tourists on the sidewalks. Guests were given masks on their way into the reception—where the colors were purple, green and gold, of course—for traditional New Orleans cuisine, followed by king cake, beignets and chicory coffee.

Each table represented one of the major krewes, like Bacchus, Orpheus and Endymion—with appropriately themed goodies, of course, like decorated coconuts for the Zulu table—making the entire reception quite possibly the gaudiest thing he'd ever witnessed.

He'd put his foot down though, at Callie's suggestion to dress him up like Rex—mainly because he was convinced it was Callie's subtle revenge for something he'd done in his youth—but did finally acquiesce to a simple black mask at Jamie's pleadings.

It was loud, ostentatious and so meta his brain wanted to explode, but it was definitely one hell of a party. *It was only going to get better, too,* he thought evilly.

And Jamie, who looked as though she was on her way to be coronated by Rex himself in her over-the-top gown, was simply incandescent with happiness. He liked to think at least a little of that was because of the actual getting-married part of the day, but Jamie's complete love of all things Mardi Gras might just be outweighing that at the moment.

She'd ditched her heavy headdress hours ago, and her cheeks were flushed pink with excitement and exertion from dancing. When the music switched to a slow song, Jamie pulled him to the floor.

"I love you."

"And I love you."

"And I know this is really not your thing," she said, "but thank you for not squashing it."

"As long as you're happy and having a good time. I'm just happy to be married."

Jamie rose up onto her tiptoes to kiss him. "So am I. And look at it this way, Callie's other idea was a Cinderella theme with pumpkins and glass slippers and God only knows what else. It could have been far worse."

"Yes, that would have been worse."

"I tell you what. Ten years from now we'll have an anniversary party and you can pick the theme. Wizards, aliens, zombies, dragons, whatever. How's that?"

"I don't think I can wait that long."

Jamie looked at him, confused. "What do you mean?"

He glanced at his watch. "Almost time."

"Almost time for what?"

He kissed her on the forehead as the music stopped and the dancing came to a confused halt. "You love me, right?"

"Of course." Her look turned suspicious. "Colin Raine, what have you done?"

"Just added my own little touch to the wedding. You got your inner geek indulged, so I indulged mine, too."

The unmistakable opening chords of "Thriller" blared out of the speakers. Jamie's eyes went wide as understanding dawned. *"No,"* she breathed in horror. "You *didn't.*"

Zombies crashed through the doors.

* * * * *